RAWHEAD BLOODYBONES

A MISSOURI LEGEND

WRITTEN BY
P.G. SWEARNGIN

ILLUSTRATIONS BY
NATHEN REYNOLDS

ISBN-10: 1463762275
ISBN-13: 978-1463762278

DEDICATION

TO TRAVIS
AND
ALL THE LOST CHILDREN
TAKEN BY THE WATER.

CONTENTS

PROLOGUE

"Rawhead Bloodybones"
is a bogeyman feared by children,
and is sometimes called *"Raw head and Bloody-Bones"*,
"Tommy Rawhead", or *"Rawhead"*.
The Oxford English Dictionary cites 1550
as the earliest written appearance as
"*Hobgoblin, Rawhed, and Bloody-bone*".
The term was used "to awe children,
and keep them in subjection",
as recorded by John Locke in 1693.
The stories originated in Great Britain and spread to
North America, where the stories were common in the
Midwest and Southern United States.
Rawhead is usually said to live near ponds or rivers,
but according to Ruth Tongue in *Somerset Folklore*,
"lived in a dark cupboard, usually under the stairs.
If you were heroic enough to peep through a crack
you would get a glimpse of the dreadful,
crouching creature, with blood running down his face,
seated waiting on a pile of raw bones that had belonged
to children who told lies or said bad words."

In the Ozarks of Missouri,
there is an account of a razorback hog named
"Rawhead" that is butchered
and the bones later reanimated by a conjuring witch.

This is the story of *Rawhead Bloodybones*
and the Battle of Lexington, a Missouri legend,
as told to the author when he was very young.

1   A STORM IS COMING

Lightening crackled and split the night sky. The first drops of rain sizzled in the fire. "Storm's a comin'," said Gramps, "might be bad."

He poked the campfire and tossed on another log. Gramps had brought the boys down to his favorite fishing spot on the banks of the Missouri River.

He had been coming there for years with his father and his grandfather. It was a special place, hard to get to but once there it was perfect, peaceful and private.

That night there were four generations camping at the secret fishing hole. Gramps, at ninety, was still as ornery as he was at seventy. He was a World War II veteran. He was shot in the ankle while storming Omaha Beach during D-Day. He was shipped out the next day and made it back home, glad to be alive but disappointed he didn't get a shot off before the Nazi's bullet took him down. Everyone thought he was going to die young. His injury caused his whole right leg to turn black from bruising and trauma after several

1

surgeries. He has outlived all four of his older brothers and still gets around just fine, as of this writing.

Pops was also a veteran. He followed in the footsteps of Gramps. Pops had retired after twenty-seven years of military service. He worked in civil service afterwards, but now mainly focuses on fishing. Pops brought his son, George, and his grandson, Benny, along with Gramps. George is a plumber and has a simple life with a wonderful wife and great son, Benny, who was now ten years old. George and Benny had also brought along their best friends to make sure everyone had a good time, which wasn't always the case when moments are shared with just family. George's friend, Mack, was an old school buddy and long time friend. Mack's son, Will, naturally became friends with Benny since the boy's fathers did most everything together, especially fishing.

That evening was a special one. They had spent the day fishing and enjoyed the early evening eating some of the day's catch just before the raindrops fell.

"Better get those tents tightened down and rain slicks ready," mumbled Gramps as he poked at the fire again. "Looks like it might be isolated," stated Pops in a bit of disagreement, not wanting to worry so much and not feeling too frisky to jump up from his comfortable perch on an old stump located the perfect distance up wind from the fire.

"Don't worry," piped in George, "it's Missouri, if you don't like the weather, wait a day and it will change."

Benny and Will didn't mind the giant raindrops and commenced to try and catch them on their tongues. Besides, they had a bit of protection from the trees they had swung their hammocks in. Ten-year-old boys don't mind the rain, on a camping trip like this, the dirtier the better. So, it was up to George and Mack to prepare the camp for the storm, just in case it got bad.

They had already pitched the tents, it was simply a matter of securing the rain fly over the top. Besides, it was an isolated summer storm and most likely would not last long. In the event of a downpour there was always the cave for protection.

The fishing hole was about one half a mile hike from the road. It was nestled along the bluffs of the Missouri River. The river had eroded inland creating a pool which collected the runoff of a small stream flowing from a cave. At the base of the bluff, there was an entrance to a cavern that meandered deep into the earth. The opening was fairly big and high enough for a grown man to stand in, but as in most caves, the floor was damp and the air was cold.

On the top of the ridge was an Indian burial mound. The Osage Indians populated this area long ago and most likely used the cave for shelter. The area was considered a sacred burial ground by the natives, but the mounds had been plundered for artifacts by prospectors many years ago.

Gramps had been fishing there for decades. His father would bring him down to the special spot and he continued to carry on the tradition.

The secret fishing hole always seemed the same. It was hallowed ground to the Indians, but to Gramps it was a unique part of the world that was always there for him.

He would recall coming to the fishing hole with his father and spoke of the thrill of "noodling" along the banks of the river.

"Did I ever take you boys noodling out here?" Gramps asked as he stoked the fire.

"No, not my idea of fishing," remarked Pops as he shifted his weight on the old stump.

George and Mack had finished prepping the camp for the storm that, at this point, seemed to be moving around them.

Of course, Ben and Will had not heard of "noodling" before. They moved closer to the fire hoping to satisfy their curiosity with a tale from Gramps.

"Ain't heard of noodling before," said Will, "what's that all about?" he inquired and Gramps smiled.

"Noodling," said Gramps, "is the most exciting, but yet most difficult way to fish. Ya see, there are some mighty big cats in this river and the best way to catch 'em is with your hands."

"Fishing with your hands?" Ben exclaimed, "That's impossible!"

Gramps chuckled, "I have caught the biggest fish of my life with these two bare hands!"

Gramps held out his arms and opened his hands. Hands worn and cracked from ages of work and fingernails containing dirt that had been there longer then the two boys had been alive.

George and Mack smiled as they rested by the fire and enjoyed the old man in his element, telling the youngsters of olden days and crazy fish stories. They had heard them many times before and yet they still seemed fresh, especially in front of a young and gullible audience.

Gramps stood and rolled up the sleeve of his shirt on his right arm. "You see these scars?" Gramps pointed up and down his arm. The boys leaned in to get a better view. There were tracks running down the length of Gramps' arm on both sides. The marks had faded over time and were not as distinguishable as they had been.

Gramps always wore long sleeved shirts, even in the hottest days of summer. If, by chance, he did get sun on his arm, the tan would reveal the scars more clearly. It seemed as if a fine-toothed comb had been scraped over his skin, shredding the flesh like a bad graze.

"You telling us a fish did that?" Will asked as he looked at his father for reassurance that Gramps was telling the truth.

"Yep, sure did," Gramps replied, "it was the second time I had to fight for my life," he embellished.

"The first time, of course, was when I was in the war. I fought the Nazi's when I was nineteen years old. I wasn't scared none...other men were peeing their pants and puking all over the boat, not me, no sir, I wasn't scared. When I fought this fish," Gramps motioned to his scarred arm, "I was fearing for my life."

A strong wind blew, breaking the boys concentration on Gramps. They looked up at the sky, searching for the storm in the darkness. The occasional lightning would reveal the thunderheads in the distance of the slow moving storm.

"Looks like it may miss us," George said.

Mack agreed.

Pops stood up to go relieve himself. "I've heard this one before," he commented under his breath.

Ben and Will both jumped up and took Pops' place on the old stump.

"Hey, I was sitting there!" Pops barked out, but the boys ignored him. The stump was closer to Gramps and they were eager to hear more about his deathly battle with a giant catfish.

"I suppose I was around the age of twenty-three," Gramps continued, "I had returned from the war with a shattered ankle and had several operations and months of physical therapy. I was told I wouldn't be able to walk again, but I would not accept that as the truth and worked hard at regaining the strength in my leg. When I was mostly healed up, my father, your great-great granddad," Gramps motioned to Ben, "brought me to this very spot to go fishing. The type of fishing he had in mind was a new experience for me, for sure. When we arrived at the spot I knew we were going fishing but we did not bring a single pole, line, hook or bait. I had no idea what he was up to. When I asked him where all the fishing gear was, he just held up his hands and said *these are all we need!*"

Gramps chuckled as he remembered that moment.

Pops returned carrying a few downed branches and placed them near the fire for future use.

"You done with your fish story there, Dad?"

"No, just getting started," replied Gramps.

"You were just getting started when I left five minutes ago," Pops commented, "I guess we don't have much better to do, so please, continue."

"Er, thanks," said Gramps, "didn't know I needed your permission," he continued sarcastically.

Pops just rolled his eyes, turned and walked over to take his place in the unoccupied hammock, just far enough away to hear but not close enough to cramp Gramps' style.

"Go on! Tell the story!" Benny and Will said simultaneously.

Gramps cleared his throat and chucked another branch on the fire from the stack Pops had just delivered.

"Noodling," continued Gramps, "is a technique of fishing that requires sheer strength and fearlessness. Qualities these men lack." Gramps swung his arm around pointing to Pops, George and Mack.

The three just laughed it off, the battles of egos had run long in this family.

Pops chimed in at the last second, "It also requires a fair level of stupidity, or maybe insanity is more like it."

Gramps pretended he didn't hear him. Selective hearing was a benefit of being a *senior* citizen. "Essentially, noodling is accomplished by swimming along creek or river banks, searching for holes in order to reach in and pull out the fish that lives there. But, it's not that simple. First, you have to be sure the hole is home to a fish and not a beaver, muskrat, otter or, worse yet, a cottonmouth."

The boys looked at each other, eyes widened.

"Generally, what you are looking for is blue cats, flatheads and the like," Gramps continued, "the trick is to feel inside the hole. If the hole goes up and out of the water, then you are noodling in the wrong house, get your arm out of there quickly!" Gramps pulled his arm back to animate his story.

"You need to find a hole that goes down and has a slimy bottom. Feel around for the smoothness in the bank. This is a good sign you've found the right hole."

The men chuckled together, sharing an inside joke that the young boys did not understand. Gramps cleared his throat again, as if to say, *knock it off,* I'm telling the story.

"Well, the day I came with my dad," Gramps went on, "he explained noodling just like I did here to you. And I was thinking the same thing you are now, but I knew I had to do it or face ridicule, and besides I was a war veteran and nothing scared me."

"We spent the better part of the morning feeling our way up and down the river bank. Some parts shallow enough to stand up in and others were deeper. Then I found it, the biggest hole so far. My dad got excited. *You just have to try your luck*, he said to me, *and hope the darn cat is in there.* I looked at him and he gave me the go ahead and motioned to the hole."

Gramps stood up to mimic his actions of that day.

"I got closer to the bank and was able to keep my head just above water."

Gramps squatted a bit to give the impression he was swimming and moving his arms around.

"I reached slowly toward the hole, felt the smooth slimy bottom and made sure it was angling down instead of up," Gramps looked at the boys, "everything was quiet and my dad gave me another nod as I looked over at him."

Gramps turned a bit as he reenacted the scene.

"I moved my hand slowly into the hole in the bank, secretly hoping there was nothing in there. I had no luck all day. I was beginning to feel like I was being led on. I had been *snipe hunting* with my dad before, only to end up as the butt of his jokes. This time it felt a little different. I had no idea."

"I moved my hand slowly into the dark slick hole. Then it happened! I felt the pain of a thousand needles pierce my arm just below the elbow. It had me and wasn't letting go! I pulled as hard as I could and felt its teeth rip down my arm to the wrist! Then I went under. The cat had clamped down even harder and pulled me farther under the water and deeper into his hole. I went limp with hopes it would let go, but to my dismay the fish reset and swallowed my arm up passed the elbow this time! At that moment I was able to place my feet on the bank and push as hard as I could with my legs. In a sudden release the fish came out of the hole, still clamped to my arm. I was flailing for breath and was able to catch a few before the sheer weight of the monster pulled me down under again!

The Big Muddy was cold and cloudy and my mind raced back to Normandy. I was sinking, the weight was too much. I was fighting to swim up and the fish was fighting to swim down. It was twisting and pulling and ripping my flesh clear around my arm! I thought for a moment if I could reach the bottom, perhaps I could walk into shallow water before I ran out of air. But the bottom wasn't coming! It was happening...my body needed air! I was no longer in control. In a final effort I kicked and surged upward and then I saw my dad's legs just above me. I reached up and grabbed his foot. He immediately reached down and grabbed me. He thrust his hand into the gills of the big cat that was still clamped to my arm. Struggling against the current, trying to find our footing, finally, we were able to pull ourselves to the bank dragging the giant fish to dry ground. Then, the cat released its grip and began flip flopping its way to the water. My dad immediately pulled out his blade and plunged it deep into the skull of the fat cat and said, *you lose!* He turned to me with a grin and said, *nice catch.*"

2 SOMETHING IN THE WATER

Lightening crackled again, the boys counted the seconds between the flash and the responding thunder.

"Four seconds," said Benny.

Gramps finished his story, "That flathead was close to four feet long and weighed near ninety-five pounds. It was bigger than you two young boys are, that's for sure."

The cloud burst began and rain started pelting down. The boys ran for the protection of their tents. They had pitched two tents, a big one for the adults and a smaller one for the two boys. George and Mack stood up and also moved toward the tents. "Gonna go grab a rain poncho," said George.

Gramps was not concerned about the rain.

"Someone might want to gather a bit more wood. We need to keep this fire going."

Pops had dozed in the hammock. After the rain started, he stood and walked over to Gramps. "Maybe we should wait till the rain passes," he said to Gramps, "go dry off a bit in the tent."

"I'm fine," Gramps replied, "someone needs to keep this fire going. Go round up the others and get me some more dry wood."

Pops turned and headed toward the tents. The boys were excited as they huddled in the doorway of their tent. "Camping is always fun, rain or shine," said Will.

"I prefer shine," Ben replied.

"Maybe we should help get some wood. It's not raining that hard."

George and Mack were just leaving their tent when Pops met them at the front.

"Got our rain gear on, so we'll get some sticks," Mack informed Pops.

"You should stick around and keep an eye on Gramps, just in case he falls in the fire," George gestured to Pops, "we won't be gone long."

Pops grunted his usual discontent to have to wait behind, although fine with not having to tromp around in the rain looking for dry wood.

Ben and Will appeared with their rain gear on.

"We are going with you," they said simultaneously.

"Ok," said George, "we are going to need flashlights and don't forget the ax."

Gramps had a tendency to drift away occasionally. When Pops approached him back at the fire he was staring into the flames as if he could see his future or perhaps his past deep within the hypnotic flickering. Gramps was mumbling indistinguishably under his breath. Pops watched him for a moment. He tried to guess what Gramps was imagining or remembering inside that old mind. There were many things Pops wanted to talk to his dad about, so many questions that were never asked. Pops was just not a kid anymore. His father's guidance wasn't needed. Besides he was a grandfather now, too. A lifetime had passed and it was just to late for those questions anymore. Gramps had lived longer than anyone expected and Pops was glad to have him around. Sadly, his relationship with Gramps was at its best now, when there is little time left, considering the amount that had already passed. Pops found himself a bit choked up as he looked at his aged father and realized how much he loved him, regardless of how they never showed each other.

He watched as his dad peered deeper into the flames. The orange glow lit the old man's face in a strange way. It cast shadows deep in the lines and wrinkles of his weathered skin. Gramps' eyes were intensely focused on the same spot in the fire. The distorted look of his face disturbed Pops, so he called out.

"You doing ok?" There was no response.

"DAD, you ok?"

"For crying out loud!" Gramps exclaimed as he snapped out of it, "why you startlin' me like that... sneakin' up and all!"

Pops said, "Boo," diverting a confrontation by turning it more into a joke.

"You can give an old man a heart attack!" Gramps continued.

"Relax or you'll give yourself one," said Pops.

The rain started to ease up as Pops bent down to pick up one of the heavier logs they had found earlier in the day.

"It's a bit wet, but we have some good coals going so it should burn, no problem." Pops slowly placed the wood over the coals.

"Yep, should be alright," Gramps agreed as he spat into the fire.

Gramps turned a can of beans he had laid on the coals on the outer edge of the fire. "Canned foods were always a tradition when camping. Cans of beans, corn beef hash, smoked oysters, anchovies, and sardines for breakfast, Of course, always bring along beef jerky and my special seasoning to use on the fish. I have a wonderful way of preparing fillets on the griddle. No matter the type of fish, I always use the same recipe. Changing it a bit here and there to fit my taste. Lemon pepper and garlic salt mixed in with my *secret* Cajun blend is the usual combination of flavors. Mix it in with some flour, dust the fillets and cook over the fire on the griddle with a bit of olive oil. Garnish with a few capers to accent the flavor and it is a mouthwatering combination."

Gramps had a habit of repeating himself. Pops knew the recipe by heart. Pops began to pick up some of the things left over from dinner. He placed the items in the cooler they had nearby. Gramps turned and stared at the fire, trying to recall a dream he couldn't remember.

George, Mack and the two boys had been gone a few moments. The trees surrounding the fishing hole provided more protection from the rain. The heat of the day had been a bit overbearing so they found the cooling rain to be a welcome reprieve. They brought with them two canvas bags to carry the wood and they each had a flashlight. Mack carried the ax. There was a path that led along the bank. It was well worn, not from constant use, but from age. Humans walked the path for centuries, but not recently, more so, by deer and other animals that lived perpetually within the forest.

Benny and Will walked together, discussing the fish story just told by Gramps. They were testing each other's bravery by daring one another into a noodling competition.

"I betcha I can catch more fish than you," challenged Will.

"I betcha you won't even go in the water," Benny responded.

George and Mack were scrounging the ground looking for dry kindling or dead tree branches. They broke a few over their knees and placed the sticks in the canvas bags.

Benny and Will kept walking further down the trail. Flashlights flailing here and there as they explored deeper into the woods.

"Don't wander off too far, you boys!" Mack yelled out as he noticed the lights moving farther away. "We have found a good bit of wood here from an old downed tree, so we may not have to look much more."

The boys kept walking with their minds full of thoughts about wrestling a giant catfish.

George and Mack had been friends since the eighth grade and were best buddies in high school. After graduation they went their separate ways. They always remained in touch and tried to get together as much as possible in the later years. Whenever they could, they would come to the river with Gramps and Pops. It had been three years since the last time.

"You know, I don't recall ever seeing signs of anyone else being here," Mack observed as he chopped on a branch.

"We don't come here too often, bound to have things come and go. It's hard to tell," George responded.

"It just always seems to be the same, not that I am complaining. I like it this way," Mack continued, "there is no trail to here from the road, yet this trail seems well worn."

Mack examined the dirt path with his flashlight.

"Do you think the animals keep it down?"

George walked over and placed a canvas bag full of broken branches and bark on the ground.

"Let's take a look," he said as he turned his flashlight to the trail. Mack and George examined the trail for footprints. "Only fresh ones are ours," George said, "looks like I see a deer track over here. Look here is a raccoon's."

"What do you think this is?" Mack pointed at a footprint in the mud, "It appears to be fairly big."

George came closer and had a look. "The track seems to be distorted in the mud like the animal slipped or something."

Mack gestured to the bigger indentation. "That looks like a big toe."

George looked at Mack. He was wondering why Mack was so concerned about this. "Mack, you are beginning to freak me out a bit. Why is this on your mind?"

Mack shook his head and started to laugh. "I don't know, just talking, I guess. It sure is nice and peaceful here. I just found it funny that there is still a place in the world that no one knows about."

George picked up the second canvas bag. "Let's get this bag full of wood and get back to camp," George motioned to Mack, "there is another dead tree just down over there."

Mack picked the ax back up and walked with George. "You doing ok? How's Will been?" George asked.

"We are getting by, I guess," Mack replied. He knew where George was going with this. "The more time that passes the better it gets, but it's something you never get over."

George nodded, "I understand."

Mack had been a truck driver for the first part of his career. He had been around the country. He had seen all he wanted and more. One particular time when he had a break, he came to visit George. George was dating a girl named Kate. He had recently met her and asked Mack to go out with them and a friend. A blind date was not Mack's idea of a good time, but he went along. He didn't know this date would change his life.

Kate's friend was named Janice and she was in nursing school. Kate was studying at the local university but had not yet decided on a major. Mack was to meet them at a local nightclub called *The Cadillac* just at the edge of town.

Mack couldn't wait to get inside the club. There was a short line at the door and he felt awkward standing alone. George, Kate and Janice were already waiting inside.

Once Mack had made it in the club, he began to look around for his old friend and the two girls he had never met. When he spotted George at the table, he admired the two girls he was with. Mack felt an overwhelming attraction, a feeling he had never felt before.

Mack checked himself over. His reflection was faintly visible in the glass of a nearby picture frame. He ran his fingers through his hair and tucked in his shirt. He took a deep breath and began to walk toward them. The twenty paces he walked seemed like eternity. He felt like he was floating rather than walking. For a second, he felt invisible, like an apparition suspended above a crowd of silent people.

George was sitting across from the two girls. All Mack could focus on was the sheer beauty of the mystery woman before him.

George stood up and said "Mack, buddy, great to see you made it," George stuck out his hand for a shake.

Mack grabbed it and pulled his friend in closer and gave him a hug. After the embrace, George turned and introduced the smiling girls. Mack swallowed and thought, *remember her name, remember her name.* He looked at the girl of his dreams and smiled. George said, "Mack, I would like you to meet, Kate."

Mack's heart dropped. Kate was George's new girlfriend. "...and this is Janice," George continued the introductions. Mack held out his hand and greeted both women. "Next round is on me," he insisted as he tried to disguise his disappointment.

It wasn't until after a few beers that Mack had the courage to approach George. He knew his feelings were strong and he wanted to know more about George's new girl.

When the girls went to the bathroom together, Mack felt it was the time to ask George about Kate.

"How long have you been dating Kate?"

"Oh, about three weeks," George replied, "She is real nice. I am just getting to know her a bit better," George took a drink of beer.

"Are you serious?" Mack inquired.

"Not yet, a bit early for that don't you think?"

Mack smiled.

"So, do you mind if I ask her to dance?"

"Not one bit," said George. George had no idea he just gave away his girl.

When Kate and Janice returned Mack stood up and immediately grabbed Kate's attention.

"May I have this dance?"

Kate looked over at George.

"Go for it," George smiled.

That was all it took. George never danced with Kate again. By the end of the evening, the bar had closed and the couples were dancing in the street.

They had switched partners and it didn't seem to bother anyone.

It was a quick romance. Mack and Kate were married a few months later. George was their best man. Mack settled down and stopped driving trucks. Kate continued her education and went on to achieve a Doctorate in Sociology. Not too long after graduation, Kate gave birth to Will. It was a good marriage.

When Will was around three years old, he became very ill. A severe strain of influenza was going around and unfortunately, the young toddler caught it. Two weeks of the flu and Will finally seemed to be getting better, and then Kate got worse. She picked up the virus from her son and didn't think it was that serious. She had the typical cough and symptoms and expected it to clear out. As the illness slowly progressed, it was clear to Mack and Kate that it had become serious when Kate woke up early one morning and her skin was blue. Her body was running low on oxygen. Mack rushed her to the hospital only to discover she had chronic pneumonia.

She died the next day. It was an unexpected turn of events that would change Mack's life forever.

Over eight years had passed since that day and George knew Mack still carried that burden with him. He was always there for Mack if he ever needed a friend to talk to. Although, George knew his friendship could not replace true love. Mack lost his soul mate and a part of him has been missing ever since.

Benny and Will had strolled down the trail. The path began to turn toward the river and edged sideways down the bluff to the water's edge. As the trail leveled out it followed along a small tributary that dumped into the big river. The pathway continued until it stopped at the edge of a small pool created as the smaller creek merged with the Missouri. The boys stopped. They realized this was where they would have to cross the water if they continued on.

"Looks like the end of the road. We had better get back, anyway," said Benny.

Will looked back toward camp. He could hear the sound of someone chopping wood. "They're still getting wood. We have time," Will smiled.

"Time for what?" asked Ben warily.

Will walked to the edge of the water and began shining his flashlight along the bank.

"Maybe we can catch a big cat and take it back to camp," he said enthusiastically.

Ben's eyes widened and he responded, "You're crazy, I'm not getting in the water."

"I knew you would be scared!" Will continued to search the waterline with his flashlight.

"Come on, Will, we need to get back. We will get in big trouble if we go in the water without our dads," Ben pleaded.

Will ignored him as he considered the possibilities of surprising everyone with a big cat.

Although it was dark and a bit rainy, Will could see fairly well without the flashlight so he handed it to Ben.

"Shine both the lights at the water and I will go in. It doesn't look too deep here. I will have to wade out a bit and look for a hole," he said as he advanced toward the edge.

"Are you sure you want to do this? You'll get all wet!"

"I am already wet!" Will said as he removed his poncho and shirt. "Just follow me with the lights and it will be ok."

Will was a bit older and slightly bigger than Ben. He was usually the leader so it was only natural that Ben did not stop him from going further with his idea. Will waded slowly into the water. The tributary flowed into the main channel and caused a small swirling current that created the circular pool. The current was not overpowering and so Will pushed forward slowly.

"Will, let's go back to camp. I think they have stopped chopping and maybe looking for us," Ben attempted once again to get Will to change his mind.

"Shhhh, you'll scare the fish!"

Will moved to the deeper side of the water along the opposite bluff from which Ben was standing.

"Shine the light over here."

Ben pointed the flashlights toward the sound of Will's voice. He could see Will was getting deeper as the water level was almost over his shoulders.

Will was approximately a foot away from the bank as he began to feel along its muddy wall.

Ben moved closer to the water's edge to get a better view and to cast some better light on his friend.

"Hurry up! I want to go back! If you don't get out of there, I am going to leave you in the dark!" Ben attempted one last time. Will wasn't listening. Ben could see the back of Will's head as it stuck up out of the water, then it disappeared.

Ben called out, "Will? Will, what are you doing? Will!" Ben clamored down to the water's edge shining the lights in the direction where Will had been. The ripples from the water reassured him he was looking in the right spot. "Will!! Come up out of the water! If this is a joke, it's not funny!" Ben began to panic. One moment his friend was there and in an instant he was gone.

3 DEATH IS ONLY THE BEGINNING

George and Mack had finished filling the second canvas bag full of wood. They had also gathered some larger chunks of driftwood and had carried the pieces to the edge of the trail. The two friends had always been able to share their deepest thoughts and philosophies. Even though they didn't always agree, they never angered each other.

"I think that should be enough wood to get us through the night," George motioned to Mack to move a little closer and he placed his hand on his shoulder. "Death is only the beginning," George looked him in the eye, "your spirits will meet again one day. In the meantime, you need to enjoy your life in this body as long as you can."

"Thanks my friend," Mack paused, "you know I am getting too old to believe in fairytales," Mack smiled at George long enough to make him smile back. "That is one thing we never have agreed on," George shrugged.

The scream that came next made the hair stand up on the back of Mack's neck. It was Benny. They both started running down the trail.

"WIIILL!!" Benny was screaming as loud as he could.

"WIIILLLL!" Benny scrambled back up from the water's edge and ran with all his might to find his dad.

They nearly collided as the trail bent back inland. When Benny saw his dad he instantly began to cry.

"Will went into the water and he didn't come back up!" Benny started to breakdown. He was scared and he knew he was in big trouble.

"Where!?" yelled Mack as he kept running down the path. Benny rushed them over to the edge of the water and pointed his flashlight at the area where Will went under.

"He was trying to noodle along the bank over there and he went under and hasn't come up!"

Without hesitation Mack rushed into the water.

Pops and Gramps just finished eating the beans they had cooked on the fire. They had begun to wonder what was taking the others so long. They heard Benny yelling for Will faintly in the distance.

"You hear that?" Gramps looked up at Pops.

"Yes," Pops confirmed as he stood up to listen harder.

"Sounds like they might be playing around."

Gramps was silent for a moment. He stood up with a grim look on his face. "No, this doesn't feel right."

The water was cold and felt extremely unwelcoming as Mack strode through. His mind whirling with thoughts and a sense of helplessness.

"Light!" he yelled as he tried to focus on the dark riverbank. "Will! Where are you?"

Mack's eyes frantically searched everywhere. He peered into the depths of the cold water, took a deep breath and went under.

At that same instant, there was the sound of splashing and flailing coming from downstream toward the main river. George and Benny ran toward the sound. Ben yelled for Will again and George searched the water with the light. As George ran closer to the water's edge, nearer the source of the sound, he saw something in the water, a flash of movement blurred by the refraction in the water. A shadowy figure was moving quickly toward the open channel and within an instant; the prevailing current swept it out of sight.

Mack resurfaced gasping for breath. He was not too far from where George and Benny had stopped.

"We saw something over there!" George yelled as he pointed the flashlight to the spot, "then it disappeared!"

Mack searched along with them as they shined the lights in the area.

"It's been too long!" Mack cried out as he began realizing how much time had passed. No one could survive being under water for this much time.

Out of the corner of his eye he saw his biggest fear come true. There was Will's limp body swirling in the vortex of the current. He was face down and slightly under the surface.

Mack had to refocus. His eyes telling him what he saw but his mind did not believe it.

"Please be a log," he thought.

No, it was unmistakably William.

By the time they arrived, Gramps and Pops were completely out of breath. They had heard the commotion and hurried down the trail as fast as their aged bodies could take them.

Wailing was the best way to describe it, the primal scream that comes from the deepest, darkest place in a man's heart. Before them, along the edge of the trail, lay Will's lifeless body. Mack was kneeling over him, soaking wet, out of breath and wailing hysterically. George and Benny were attempting to save Will's life.

"Keep up the compressions, Benny," George said has he removed his mouth from Will's. Benny began to cry as his father looked at him.

Pops stood for a moment to take in what was happening before him. His first instinct was to calm Mack down. "It's gonna be ok. Quiet down."

Then Gramps yelled, "Kick'em in the lungs! You gotta kick'em in the lungs!" Gramps hurried over, "turn him on his side!"

"What?" George wasn't sure what he was talking about. He rolled Will's body on its side with his back facing Gramps.

Gramps positioned himself and with the side of his foot, kicked William hard in the back. He did it again.

Water came spewing out of Will's mouth. He began frantically coughing and gasping for air.

"Turn him upside down!" Gramps yelled.

Mack and George grabbed William by the ankles and swiftly held him upside down. Another burst of water gushed out of his mouth.

"Ok, that should do it!" yelled Gramps.

Will continued to cough and gasp as they set him down.

"He may go into shock!" Gramps continued, "We need to get him back to camp!"

Mack cradled Will in his arms and hurried back down the path to their camp.

Mack was out of view when the others came up to the pile of wood and canvas bags they had filled earlier.

"I need to stop here anyway, my legs just can't keep up," said Pops. Gramps stopped along with him and bent over to catch his breath.

"We will bring the bags, because we are going to need wood!" Pops yelled over to George and Benny. He nodded to them to indicate they should catch up with Mack.

When the old men arrived back at camp, the boys had laid out a palette of blankets by the fire for Will. They had covered him up and Mack was hunched over him constantly checking his breathing.

"We need to get him to the hospital!" George yelled out as he saw his dad and grandfather approaching.

"No, he'll be ok!" Gramps responded.

"How do you know that?" George asked him.

Gramps looked him in the eye. "I've seen it before. As I was lying on Omaha beach, my ankle shattered into bits, I watched dozens of our boys wash up on the shore. I could have sworn they were all dead. There was nothing I could do. I was down, leg numb. I crawled on my hands and knees to a small bomb crater and watched helplessly. The medics would risk their lives and rush out to the drowned soldiers, turn them on their sides and kick the lungs out of them. They saved a few lives that way, but not all. Give it a moment, Will should be ok."

They gathered around Will. Pops placed more wood on the fire. The rain seemed to be over and fortunately, there were enough coals to reignite the fire.

Mack had regained his composure and looked over at Benny. "What just happened out there?"

Benny looked at his dad and began to cry.

"It's ok, son, you are not in any trouble," George reassured him.

"It was a flathead!" Benny cried out. "I told Will not to do it. I couldn't stop him. He wanted to try noodling so he went in the water. It must have been a giant flathead that took him down. One second he was there and then he went under. I thought he was playing a trick on me!" Benny continued crying.

"Do you think a fish could really do that?" Mack asked as he looked over at Gramps. Mack had never really believed the fish stories the old man told.

"I s'pose if it were big enough and the boy's little enough," Gramps pointed over to Will, "take a look at his arms and see if it left any marks."

Mack began to uncover Will.

At that moment, Will opened his eyes.

"Dad!"

Mack embraced him.

"I'm here, son, I am here."

Mack began to choke up.

"What happened? I thought I lost you."

William looked up at his father. His eyes glazed over and he paused a moment to remember.

"Was it a fish?" Benny knelt down beside his friend. Will looked around at all of them and said, "No, it was a ...man."

They were all quiet. The fire crackled as the flames bit a new log. William stared into the fire, his eyes widened as he recalled what had just happened to him.

"I was along the riverbank and about to put my hand in a hole I had found. I was nervous. Then he grabbed me by my legs and pulled me down! He held me under water...he was trying to drown me!"

The men all looked at each other. Concern grew as they glanced around the campsite.

"Are you sure that's what happened? Could it have been a tree limb or something that caught your leg?" Mack asked his son.

"No! It was alive!" Will began to choke up, "I-I saw eyes...big red eyes. His head was..." Will paused.

"Well, it was bloody and raw! It looked like I could see his brains! And his skin, it was...it was...melted...dripping off the bones!"

A sudden recollection overcame Gramps and he muttered, "Rawhead."

4 RAWHEAD

Pops was the only one who heard Gramps. He walked over to him and whispered in his ear.

"You can't be serious."

Gramps looked at him with deep concern on his face. "George, Mack, you two should go get the rest of the fire wood we left on the trail. I think we are going to need it," Gramps pointed at the fire.

George looked up at his grandfather. "What we need is to get this boy to a hospital. He could die here!"

"No!" Gramps insisted, "I have seen many soldiers recover just fine after being filled up with sea water. Besides, it is too dangerous to leave camp *now*. We need to wait until dawn."

Mack had finished examining Will for marks or abrasions.

"You just have some bruising around your legs. Are you sure you didn't get tangled up in some debris, Will?" Mack looked at his son, hoping for a better explanation.

Will was exhausted and had drifted off. Mack stood up and turned to George.

"Apparently, Will is delusional. It's to be expected, I guess. We should go get that wood because we need to talk."

"We'll be right back," George assured Benny as they began to head toward the trail. They picked up the empty canvas bags as they headed out. When George and Mack were out of hearing distance from the others they began to speak.

"What do you think is going on, George?"

"I can't be sure. When you were underwater searching for Will, Benny and I saw a figure moving downstream from where Will was found. We couldn't make it out. It could have been a large fish or a distorted tree limb or...a man. The strange thing was, it was moving quickly, retreating toward the swifter current. Then you reappeared and spotted Will and I have disregarded it until now."

They had walked down the trail and came to the remaining wood they had gathered earlier.

"Whatever is going on, I think we still need to get out of here as soon as we can. Get Will checked out, just to be sure he is ok," George said as he placed the bigger chunks of wood into the bag. "Let's just get enough to fill these bags and get back to camp."

Gramps pulled Pops aside and whispered, "we need to talk somewhere without startling the boys."

"Ok, let's go in the tent," replied Pops, "Benny, stay with Will and do not leave his side. We are going to the tent."

Once they were in the tent, Pops laid into Gramps.

"What were you thinking? Rawhead!? I am sure glad they didn't hear you," Pops glared at Gramps, "those boys are already frightened enough, the last thing you need to do is add to it with your stories."

"It's not *my* story," Gramps retorted, "the boy described him almost exactly. How would he know?"

"Rawhead Bloodybones is a myth! Plain and simple. There must be an obvious explanation for what happened here and I don't know why you are insisting we stay. We need to get out of here and the sooner the better."

Gramps just grunted. He stared down at the floor of the tent.

"It's too dangerous, Francis."

Francis was Pops real name and when Gramps said it, Pops knew he was serious. He never called him Francis. Pops hated that name and held it against his father for naming him that. Even though Gramps had apologized numerous times and insisted that it was a popular man's name at the time he was born. Pops went by *Frank* most of the time until Benny was born and once he became a grandfather, everyone called him *Pops*.

"Dad, I think you are crazy or possibly senile. I remember the story you told me about Rawhead and it's right up there with Big Foot and the Loch Ness Monster," Pops shook his head in disbelief.

"I haven't heard much about him in years," Gramps said as he pondered the existence of Rawhead, "everything fits. The boy described him exactly...his preferred method of murder...is drowning...it's very hard to doubt this is what we are dealing with."

"Come on, Dad! I can't believe you are actually saying what you are saying!" Pops grabbed Gramps by the shoulders and tried to shake some sense into him.

It was hard to accept, but Pops found himself trying to remember the story of Rawhead Bloodybones and if it were true...how it could be possible.

George and Mack arrived back at camp with the wood. They noticed right away that Gramps and Pops were no longer near the fire. Benny was sitting next to Will. Will still had his eyes closed as he lay on the blankets.

"Where are the old men?" Mack asked.

"They went to the tent," Benny replied as he looked up at them. They could see the concern in Ben's eyes.

"It's going to be ok. Will is going to be ok. We will be leaving here soon," George reassured him.

It was close to midnight and sunrise was several hours away. George was not planning on staying that long and he needed to convince Gramps it was time to go.

When George and Mack reached the big tent they could hear the conversation inside.

"Besides," Pops was saying, "he never was reported to be seen around these parts, usually further east, near the big bend, that's more than a hundred miles from here."

"He travels the river, always has," replied Gramps, "never been too far away from it, that's for sure."

George pulled the tent flap back as he entered.

"*What* or should I say *who* are you talking about?" George inquired as Mack followed him in.

Gramps and Pops stared at the other two. They did not want to explain. It was unfortunate their conversation was over heard.

"You are not going to believe this, but Gramps here thinks Will was attacked by *Rawhead Bloodybones*," Pops reluctantly admitted.

"What the hell is that?" questioned Mack.

"You really don't want to know," said Gramps.

The men returned to the safety of the fire. The boys were both asleep, exhausted from the days events.

Benny could not fight the sleep that had overcome him and he lay on the palette next to Will.

"This had better not be one of your fairy tales," said Mack as they all gathered around Gramps to hear what he had to say.

"Well then, you are going to be disappointed because that is *exactly* what it is," replied Pops.

"I have heard this one, too," George added, "there was talk of *Rawhead* when those neighborhood boys disappeared years ago. You know, Travis and the others, I can't remember. I just recall a rumor going around that *Rawhead got'em*."

Gramps settled back into his chair. They had plenty of wood on the fire and the boys were sleeping.

"Ok, I will tell you what I know," Gramps whispered as he looked up at the sky and wondered where to begin.

"I suppose I will start at the beginning."

Gramps turned and looked at the other three.

"It's a long old story and I will try to recall it all, but like I said, it has been a long time, so bear with me. My grandfather told me the story when I was just a kid, and he swore every word of it was true...

The young man's name was *Tommy* and later called *Rawhead Bloodybones*, due to his horrific appearance...the conditions of which I will explain momentarily..."

5 THE ORIGIN OF EVIL

Tommy was born into a poor family that lived in Kentucky or possibly Tennessee. His father scraped by as a fur trader and trapper. They farmed a little tobacco and grew crops mainly for subsistence living. His father and mother, along with two sisters, mostly kept to themselves.

The War Between the States had begun and families were moving west to avoid being caught in the middle of the turmoil between the North and South. Tommy's father was stubborn and refused to leave his property. It was all he had. Tommy's family was too poor to own slaves and didn't want any part in fighting over them. Not much is known about them and people reckon they had no other place to go.

Tommy was the youngest in the family. He was a skinny lad, stronger than he looked. In his late teenage years, he appeared older than he was due to the harsh conditions of the farm. He was taught how to farm, trap and skin animals by his father and two older sisters. He grew very adept at it. His father wanted more boys to help around the farm. Tommy being the third child and the only boy made it harder for him. Unable to afford slaves, the lack of sons irritated his father.

Their father worked them all very hard and was extremely angered when Tommy accidentally injured his left hand while setting a large steel foothold trap. The trap sprung prematurely while he was trying to set it. Its jaws crushed all four fingers in his left hand. The injury caused his fingers to become deformed and twisted. It also enraged his father. The injury would set them back several days on the farm. Due to the extreme frustration of his father and for fear of her son's life, Tommy's mother punished her son by sending him to the woodshed to sleep for three nights. By doing so, it revealed her discontent and separated Tommy from her husband, which prevented further beatings of her son at the hands of a raging father.

On the eve of the third night, the family had finished dinner and Tommy was directed to the woodshed where he would sleep for the final night of his punishment. Once he arrived at the woodshed, he knew his father would come out to finish up some of the evening chores, and so, in fear of a beating, Tommy shut the door and hoped for the best. He pressed his face against the backside of the door, peered through the slit in the wood and watched as his father walked out on the front porch and gathered what he needed to finish skinning a raccoon they had trapped the night before.

There was a tree in the front yard that his father used to skin animals. It had a low hanging branch on which he had hung a rope. At the bottom of the rope were two large metal hooks bent out in opposite directions. The hooks were used to pierce between the tendons of the raccoons back legs. The raccoon hung upside down as his father began skinning the animal. He cut the hide around each of the ankles and then brought the knife along the inside of each leg, down toward the rectum. Another cut was made perpendicular and up the raccoons tail about three inches. His father started peeling the hide away from the animals flesh. After the legs and tail were skinned, the hide was pulled down and removed, not unlike pulling off a wool sweater.

It was twilight, that moment of grey just before darkness. An eerie silence overcame Tommy as his father stopped what he was doing and gazed down the narrow dirt road that led up to their house. Tommy adjusted his position in the woodshed so he could get a better view of what caught his father's attention. In the distance, as the sunlight faded, appeared a silhouette of several men on horseback. As the shadowy riders approached, his father slipped the skinning knife in its sheath and started walking back to the front porch.

"Maw! We got visitors," Tommy's father yelled out, "best ya'll kept hid inside 'til I see what they want."

The riders had arrived rather quickly after they spotted the old man heading toward his house. Tommy watched from the woodshed as his father reached the top step of the front porch and turned to face the advancing riders.

They were Union soldiers. Six of them, dressed in clean uniforms and armed with muskets. The commander of the group rode up a bit closer and dismounted. He slowly walked toward the house, musket in hand and eyes glued on Tommy's father.

"Are you lost?" Tommy's father asked as he tried to size up the officer and get a feel for his intentions.

"No, sir, we know exactly where we are," said the commander as he walked up the steps of the home, placing him at eye level with Tommy's father.

"In that case, you realize you are trespassing on private property," his father quickly replied as he began to realize this was not going to be a pleasant visit from these unexpected strangers.

"You may be correct, at least for the moment," the commander added, "I am Colonel Patterson, we are here to negotiate possession of this land for Union purposes until further notice."

Colonel Patterson signaled to his troops to bring forward documentation to validate his claim.

"Also, we are told," the colonel continued, "you have a son that is of the right age to fight and he will be enlisted in the Union or otherwise face punishment for treason."

The colonel spat on the steps as he reached down to receive the papers that a soldier brought over to him.

"You have no right to claim anything here!" Tommy's father retorted as his anger began to build.

"I am not a slave owner and take no side in this war!"

The colonel signaled to his men to dismount and they proceeded to do so.

"Bring your wife and children outside!" the colonel ordered.

"I will do no such thing. You have no rights here! This is not subject to negotiation!" Tommy's father was enraged.

Tommy was quietly watching from the woodshed. He was concerned for his family, but knew he couldn't give himself up for fear of being forced to serve in a war he knew nothing about.

The colonel raised his musket and pointed it directly at Tommy's father. He then signaled to his troops to enter the home and retrieve the family. In a moment of confusion and disbelief Tommy's father stood by and watched as the soldiers forced the women out of the house and onto the porch.

"Where is the boy?" The colonel asked his men.

"He's not inside," a soldier responded.

"Where *is* the boy?" The colonel questioned Tommy's father.

"I sent him down to the creek to check our traps. He won't be back for quite some time," his father lied, "besides, he won't be no good to you any sort. He's gimped up his left hand and has never been all that right in the head. He's weak and not soldier material."

"I will be the judge of that! We will just wait here for him to return. In the meantime, I suggest you get your women here to fix us some vittles and bring out some water. My men are parched and are in need of a good meal."

The colonel motioned to another soldier standing below him off the porch.

"Take a look around and see if that boy ain't hiding somewhere."

Through the crack in the door Tommy could see the scout approaching the woodshed. Darkness had fallen and it was difficult to see exactly what was happening on the front porch. Tommy noticed his mother and sisters return inside the home. His father was arguing with the colonel as the scout slowly advanced toward the woodshed.

The scout arrived at the door to the woodshed. He lowered his musket and used the bayonet to lift up the latch and slowly open the door. As the door swung outward, the soldier squinted to get a better look through the darkness. The shed was empty, save for the wood that was stacked on either side. A walkway was between the stacks and the scout slowly stepped into the shed. He did not see the ax as it swung down from above him and split his forehead open.

Tommy climbed down from the rafters and slowly closed the door.

"Hurry up in there!" the colonel yelled through the door at the women as he held their father at gunpoint. Two of the soldiers stepped back inside the house to see what the delay was. The other two stood guard at the base of the steps. They watched as the colonel began to lose his patience.

"Seems a bit late to be running traps. Your boy should be back by now. I have a suspicion you're hiding him somewhere."

The colonel pressed the tip of his bayonet against the old man's chest.

"You best be calling him out soon or I can arrest you or even worse..."

The women interrupted him as they came back out on the porch. They had in their hands plates of left over fish, potatoes and bread. The two other soldiers were following close behind.

The second soldier stepped closer to the father and whispered, "After supper, I'm thinking your daughters here can give us a little dessert."

Before anyone knew what happened, Tommy's father plunged his skinning knife into the soldier's left eye. He quickly turned, lashed out and was able to slice the colonel's larynx open.

As he fell, the colonel pulled the trigger and shot Tommy's father in the stomach.

The girls screamed and dropped the dishes. They rushed to their father's side.

The remaining soldier on the porch and the two guarding the front made a feeble attempt to save their leader's life.

The colonel was lying on the porch holding his throat, gurgling profanities.

A soldier grabbed the nearest daughter by the hair and dragged her over to the dying colonel.

"Save *him*!" he screamed.

The girl placed her head between her knees and began to weep. Realizing she wasn't helping, the soldier hit her in the back of the head with the stock of his musket. He repeatedly pounded the girl's skull with a lavish vehemence.

During all the chaos, no one had noticed that the scout had returned from the woodshed. He stood at the base of the stairs, raised his musket and fired. The soldier who was beating the girl dropped to the floor, dead.

The two guards, who were attending to the colonel, turned around and met their doom as the scout stabbed them both in the chest with his bayonet.

He then stood over the colonel and thrust the bayonet deep into the leader's heart. He repeatedly stabbed the man multiple times, his anger boiling up to the point of insanity.

The scout walked over to the woman who was weeping over her dead husband. He grabbed her hair and pulled her head up, forcing her to look at him, and then he said, "goodbye, mother."

6 A TASTE OF MURDER

Tommy never saw his mother again. He left her on the porch with his sisters and dead father. He mounted the colonel's horse and galloped away without looking back.

Tommy raced through the night, putting as much distance between him and the slaughtered Union soldiers. The uniform he was wearing was slightly big. He did not know how long he could keep up this disguise. Aware he was representing himself as a Union soldier, he was not sure if that was in his best interest. At dawn, he slowed his pace and decided to get off the main road. He knew he needed to continue going west. So, with the rising sun to his back, he began to break a new trail into the forest ahead of him.

It wasn't long before he realized it would be difficult to continue on horseback. When he came to a small creek, he decided to turn the horse loose and continue on foot, along the water's edge. Since he had no other clothing, he kept the uniform on with intent on changing at his first opportunity.

Tommy did not know much about the war. He assumed he should avoid all contact with outsiders. Word would soon spread of the murdered Union troops and eventually, he assumed, he would be a wanted man. Disguised as a Union soldier could also get him killed by a Confederate. He had very few options.

Several hours had passed and the sun was growing higher in the sky. Tommy had become weary and decided to rest. He had been following the creek as much as possible, continuing west as far as he could tell. He came upon a small island where the water split and continued around both sides of a sand bar. In the middle, there was a snag and a large pile of debris that had collected around it. It reminded him of a beaver dam and he chose to rest inside the tangled mess of tree limbs.

It was dark by the time he awoke to the sound of a barking dog. Then he heard a voice:

"What you got there, dog? Have you found some dinner?"

Tommy opened one eye slightly to see where the voice was coming from. The dog was only a few feet away, barking directly at him. An old hermit was approaching with a torch in his hand. Tommy could see the flame flickering. The orange light created shadows that danced inside the wood debris.

"Well look there, seems to be a dead Union soldier washed up in them sticks." The hermit spoke to his dog. "He doesn't seem too ripe. Ain't been dead fer long..."

Tommy played dead as he wondered what to do next.

The dog barked and whined and wagged its tail. It was a thin mixed breed, which obviously had not had a good meal in quite a while. The hermit wasn't much different. Old and thin and starving, they had come to the creek in search for food and were excited about the opportunity to eat Tommy.

The hermit did not expect the corpse to come to life when he began lifting the driftwood out of the way.

"Raaaaaah!"

The scream startled the hermit as well as the dog. Tommy rushed to his feet and tackled the hermit around the waist. The hermit's torch went flying. The dog repeatedly bit Tommy on the leg. Tommy shoved the hermit into the water. He used the advantage of surprise to easily overcome the hermit. The old man was flailing to get out of the water. Tommy wrestled him down and wrapped his arm around the hermit's neck, submerging him under the water.

Tommy held the hermit under the water until the last bubbles of breath left the old man's nose and his body went limp.

As Tommy dragged the old man out of the water and onto the sand bar, the scrawny dog clamped down on the back of Tommy's calf. The pain shot up his leg. He reached down and grabbed the dog by the scruff of the neck. The dog was determined not to let go, so Tommy dragged the dog into the water. The dog released its grip. Tommy threw himself on top of the dog and pushed the animal down under the water. The dog's claws ripped into his chest and arms. Tommy held the dog under and tightened his grip around its throat. The dog quivered and made one last attempt to take a breath and with that, the animal became still and lifeless.

Tommy pulled the dog up out of the water and dropped it next to its master. He collapsed beside the dead bodies. His left hand was throbbing due to the injury from the trap. His blood was trying to circulate through the distorted fingers and caused a considerable amount of pain. He rested along side the two corpses until the pain subsided.

Tommy sat up after a few moments and rummaged through the old hermit's pockets. He discovered a small pouch tied to the old man's belt. Inside there was some fishing line, rusty hooks and an old hunting knife. Tommy took off the water soaked uniform he was wearing and undressed the hermit. He decided to take the old man's clothes even though they were old and raggedy.

After he dressed himself in the old hermit's clothes, Tommy smelled smoke. He hadn't noticed the hermit's torch had landed inside the pile of debris and wood on the sand bar. The torch ignited some dry leaves that had accumulated in the large pile and the smoke was increasing. It wasn't long before the large pile was burning quite rapidly.

Tommy took the small knife in his hand and leaned over the old dog. The pains of hunger had now taken over. He began to skin the animal just as his father taught him. After he removed the dog's hide, Tommy dragged the body into the water and slit its guts open. He reached into the carcass and pulled out the organs and sent them down stream with the current.

Tommy picked up a large tree branch from the creek bank and shoved one end inside the dog's rib cage. He then propped the dog carcass over the fire. The smell of the dog's burning flesh made Tommy's stomach rumble. He had never eaten dog before and assumed it would taste much like squirrel or raccoon, which he had eaten plenty of. The fire grew larger and it wasn't long before the intense heat had cooked the meat thoroughly.

The dog was delicious.

The fire was beginning to burn even bigger. The large pile of debris on the sand bar was full of old dry driftwood and leaves that had been trapped for years. Tommy decided it was time to move on for fear of being discovered. He picked up the Union uniform and tossed it onto the bonfire. He walked over to the dead hermit. He picked the old man up and threw the dead body over his shoulder. Tommy got as close to the raging fire as he could and heaved the dead hermit into the flames. The fire roared and hungrily consumed the corpse. Tommy picked up the dog's hide and tossed it on the fire. The sizzling hair put off a stench that made Tommy gag. He bent down and put the hermit's hunting knife and fishing gear into a pocket on the raggedy britches and walked away.

Tommy continued west as best as he could determine. He followed the creeks and streams as much as possible. He knew he would eventually come to the mighty Mississippi River. Once there, he would have to make a decision. Civil war was all around and he knew the big river would be full of people and danger. He did his best to avoid contact with anyone.

It was several days of traveling that would end up taking him to the river's edge. The dog he ate many days ago was long gone and the growing pain of hunger started again.

Tommy slept along the river's edge for several nights. He ate earthworms and did his best to fish with the worms he didn't eat. One morning he was awakened by the sound of a steamboat heading up river. The boat was fascinating to Tommy, having never seen one before. He heard the men sounding off the depth of the water every few seconds. The noise from the steamer was getting louder and he realized it was coming closer to the riverbank.

Tommy watched as the steamer slowed and the big paddle wheels turned. The pilot was veering off course to avoid a huge snag that was well marked due to the fact it had claimed the life of a steamer not so long ago. Tommy could hear the men calling out to each other but could not make out what they were saying. The men were extremely focused on the navigation and Tommy felt this might be a perfect time to get a ride.

Hunger had control over him to the point he was willing to risk anything in hopes of getting something to eat. How he was going to get aboard was yet to be determined. He studied the ship, looking for a place to climb on. The steamer was very large and full of supplies and merchandise. Along the starboard side there was a small rope dangling in the water. How secure it would be was unknown, but Tommy felt it was his only chance to get aboard. The ship came a bit closer, corrected its course and began to speed up. Tommy decided to follow it up stream for several miles. He needed to get ahead of it in order to swim out far enough in advance and wait for the ship to come to him.

Tommy swam out to the middle of the channel. The current was taking him down river, while the steamer was paddling up river. To avoid being spotted, he sunk down below the surface and waited for the ship to go by. He could hear the giant paddlewheels churning the water. The hull appeared above him as it slowly cut through the river. He came up directly under the steamer. The side paddlewheels pulled him in both directions. The roiling paddles were like giant teeth cutting through the water.

RAWHEAD

As the steamer passed over him, he felt his lungs begin to burn. He was running out of air. Fighting the swirling current, Tommy kicked his way to the stern of the ship. He resurfaced just as the hull cleared way above him. He gasped for breath. The wake of the giant steamer forced him down river. The distance between him and the ship's stern was increasing. He was weakening by the second. Hunger and exertion had taken all the energy he had. He looked up and watched the steamer slowly drift away. Frustrated, he gave one last attempt to swim after it. Fighting against the current was very difficult. Just as he was about to give up, he noticed the dock line he had seen earlier from the shore. It was trailing behind the steamer at a length of about thirty feet. The end of the rope was not far away and with a renewed energy he was able to catch up to it. He grabbed on with both hands. He took up the slack and the rope became taut. It was secured to a cleat on the starboard side nearer the stern. Tommy slowly began pulling his way toward the steamboat.

Undetected, Tommy was able to pull himself up and climbed on the rear deck of the steamer. The crews' attention was mainly forward of the boat and this allowed Tommy to sneak on board.

The steamboat was one hundred and seventy feet long and thirty feet wide. It carried a smaller crew because it was full of freight and merchandise heading for St. Louis, Missouri. Tommy found his way to a small aft cabin and slipped inside. It looked to be currently unoccupied. It had a bed, washbasin and bed pan. He was overcome with fatigue. He turned and shut the cabin door and locked it from the inside. The bed was so inviting, he didn't care about the risk he was taking by being a stowaway. He laid his aching body down. He could hear the big wheels churning and the constant chugging of the steam engine, the sound was hypnotizing. His mind began to wonder what would happen next. His concern was overpowered by his exhaustion. He closed his eyes and sleep took him.

The hours passed. Tommy was unsure how long he slept. When he awoke it was dark and a dense fog had swept over the river. He heard the steam engine and the mighty paddlewheels keeping a slow and steady pace. The ship's whistle was blasting and it took him a moment to recall where he was.

He tried to rise but the pain in his body prevented it. His left hand was throbbing and his legs were very stiff. The back of his leg was bruised and the punctures from the dog's teeth were oozing. The hermit's old cotton shirt was still damp and was stuck to the scabs that had formed over the deep scratches on his chest. He began to remove the old clothing he had taken from the hermit. He struggled to remove the leather boots he had kept from the soldier. The hermit did not have shoes. The pain and stiffness was almost unbearable as he bent down to remove the boots. Tommy stood and with a quick jerk, pulled the shirt up over his head. The shirt took with it the scabs that had bled into the cotton, causing him to cry out. He placed the clothes on the floor and began to wash his wounds with a small cloth and a little water he found at the bottom of an old jug that was sitting next to the washbasin.

Hunger was what he felt next. It seemed to always be there, but this time it was overwhelming.

Tommy took the blanket from the bed and wrapped himself in it. He picked up the boots and clothes and carried them over to the door. He reached inside the trousers and took out the small hunting knife; grateful he had not lost it in the river. Draped in the blanket, knife in hand and the boots and clothes tucked under his arm, he slowly opened the cabin door. The cool air came flowing in from the walkway. He slowly looked out and was relieved to see no one. He quickly walked to the side of the boat and dropped the clothes and boots into the river. Staying in the shadows, he crept around the ship's aft looking for anything to eat.

Hoooot! Hoooot! It was the ship's whistle and it startled Tommy. He ducked inside a passageway forward of the little cabin he had just slept in. The corridor led him down to a door. He tried to open the door. He rattled the latch. It was locked.

His heart began to race as he heard footsteps coming along the deck. He could not tell which direction the feet were headed. He closed his eyes and listened intently. The footsteps were getting closer. Tommy squatted down and pulled the blanket over his head and held his breath. Through a small hole in the blanket, he saw a man stumble past the darkened corridor in which he was hiding. The man continued further aft toward the little cabin where he had slept. Tommy slowly exhaled. The man fumbled with the latch and opened the door to the small cabin, stepped inside and closed the door behind him.

Suddenly, the door that Tommy was leaning on opened from the inside. Tommy fell backward into the room. Startled, he jumped up and flashed the little blade he had been carrying. A small slave boy stood before him and blankly stared.

"Don't hurts me, massah," the boy whispered.

"Silence", Tommy signaled to the boy to be quiet.

The young slave was not very old. He was naked except for a bit of cloth he had tied around his waist. His skin was dark and covered with scars, burns mostly. Around the slave's ankle was a locked clasp hooked to a chain that was bolted to a pillar in the room.

Tommy looked up at the boy's face. The slave continued to stare blankly forward.

"Don't hurts me, massah," he repeated, "I jes trying to hep, you locked out...lost key?"

Tommy slowly shut the door behind him and locked it back. He swung around and stuck the knife in front of the young boy's face. The slave just stood still. Tommy stepped closer and through the darkness he could see the young man's eyes had been plucked out of his head.

Tommy lowered his blade. He looked at the slave. He was so young and had suffered so much abuse.

"I good, now, massah, promise to always be good..." the boy whispered. "I no lie, steal no moe...please, no burns, I good now...me sorry for what I done..."

"Bastards..." Tommy muttered under his breath. "You stay quiet now..." Tommy followed the chain over to where it was bolted to the pillar. Tommy twisted the nut loose, after several attempts, and slipped the chain off the bolt.

"We goin' somewhere's right now, massah?" the slave asked nervously.

"Can you swim?" Tommy whispered.

The slave boy paused for a moment. "Who you...?"

Tommy gathered up the chain.

"Hold out your hands."

The slave slowly raised his arms up and Tommy placed the bundled chain in his hands.

"My massah, sent you to kill me...?" the slave trembled, "...I good, now, promise..." he pleaded.

"Say no more!" barked Tommy.

Tommy slipped out of the blanket and quietly led the blind slave boy out of the room and down the corridor to the ship's stern.

"Swim to your freedom or die..." Tommy whispered in the slave's ear as he pushed him overboard.

Tommy crept back to the room where he found the slave. He fell to his knees and wept for the first time since he left home.

7 SCARS OF WAR

The slave's quarters were empty, except for the pillar that the slave boy was chained and the mess of feces smeared on the floor. The stench was unbearable as Tommy stood back up and began to look around. He discovered another door on the back wall of the little room. It was cleverly built to appear as part of the wall. He pressed his ear against the door and listened for any movement. He tried the latch and noticed it was unlocked. Tommy slowly opened the door and looked into the adjoining room. What he saw next made him smile. It was a storeroom filled with supplies. Crates of canned food and new clothes were stacked to the ceiling. Jars of pickled vegetables and cases of weapons, pistols, powder, lead balls, all neatly placed before him. He opened a crate next to the door and found new boots inside. Several pairs of the richest leather boots he had ever seen. He began rummaging though the crate looking for his size. He pulled out a pair that looked like they would fit him nicely. He sat the boots down on the floor and admired them. But, his first priority was eating. He opened a jar of peaches and the smell made his mouth water. The first bite of peach was wonderful. He took another and another, the juice running down his chin. He opened another crate, green beans, then okra, corn, cucumbers. He had never eaten food that tasted this good. After a moment of frantic eating, he paused and began admiring the new clothing he found. The shirts, trousers, socks, undergarments were all new and clean. He had never worn a new shirt. His clothing had always been handmade from scraps or second hand. For a moment, Tommy had forgotten where he was. All the fine things he had discovered took him in. Tommy slowly began dressing himself in the new clothes. The fabric even smelled good. It felt soft against his skin and he thought to himself how new clothes can change the way you feel. He pulled the beautiful leather knee high boots on his legs. It was the final touch that brought back his confidence. He was revitalized.

The sound of the ship's horn startled him again and he snapped back to reality. It was the dead of night. The steamer had slowed its pace but kept chugging and churning as it crawled its way up the Mississippi.

Tommy did his best to tidy up the crates he had opened and placed everything back where it belonged. The supplies were stacked several rows deep on either side of him and the room was much bigger than he realized. In fact, he was in the bowels of the ship. The storeroom extended the full beam of the steamer. It also continued further forward until another wall separated the storeroom from the boiler room. As Tommy approached the wall, the sound of the steam engine became louder. Behind the wall, he could hear the pistons pumping, the steam hissing, wheels turning and men snoring.

"Snoring?" Tommy thought to himself.

He turned his head and pressed his ear to the wall. When he did that, he could see down the wall to the corner of the storeroom. In the shadows appeared a crewman slumped up against what seemed to be a large safe hidden in the corner of the storeroom. Tommy's eyes widened, as he stood motionless against the back wall. The crewman was snoring. He was deep in sleep. He had a pistol on his lap and his left arm was wrapped around a half empty gallon jug of water. Next to the jug was a partially eaten loaf of bread.

Tommy slowly made his way toward the sleeping crewman. He quietly weaved his way around the stacks of crates. He dropped down to his hands and knees and slowly crawled toward the crewman. He reached over and cautiously removed the pistol from the crewman's lap. Tommy quietly placed the pistol on top of the large safe that the crewman was leaning against.

Tommy knelt down in front of the man. The crewman's heart rate was very slow. His breathing was deep and the snoring resonated within his chest. Tommy removed the crewman's arm from around the jug of water. The water was clear and clean inside the glass jug and the temptation to take a drink was irresistible. Tommy lifted the jug to his mouth and took a big drink. As he swallowed, he began to feel a sensation he had never felt before. The water began to burn his mouth and throat. He could feel the liquid fire as it seared its way to his stomach. Tommy fell backwards. "Poison!" he thought. He immediately vomited.

"Har har har, hmm hmm..." the crewman laughed at Tommy as he came out of his slumber. He looked at Tommy with one eye open and his smiled revealed his gritty teeth.

"He tries to steal a drink and can't handle it. Har, har, my shine too much fer yer...? Serves ye right you bloody thief!" The crewman opened his other eye. He glared at Tommy. "Stealing me drink is one thing, robbing a man of his gun is a crime!" The crewman fumbled around for his pistol. Instead, he found the bread knife he had next to the loaf on the floor. He lashed out at Tommy and missed. Tommy swiftly grabbed the glass gallon jug and smashed it across the drunken crewman's face, breaking his nose. Blood gushed out of the man's nostrils. The crewman fell backwards. Tommy took the knife out of the man's hand and stabbed him repeatedly with it.

Tommy retrieved the blanket he had taken from the cabin and rolled the dead crewman up in it. He was still dizzy from the drink and squatted down to catch a breath. He picked up the half eaten loaf of bread and ate some. The cold night air had begun to pierce through the new cotton shirt he was wearing and he shivered. Tommy looked around and noticed the crewman's coat was hanging on a hook a little farther down the wall. It was a thick long wool coat and he slipped it on.

Tommy was searching through the pockets on the coat when he found a small silk handkerchief in the inside pocket. The material felt so smooth and rich. He took it out of the pocket and rubbed his cheek with the fine fabric. When he unfolded it to have a better look, there were numbers and letters written on it. Right 11-Left 31-Right 25. He was puzzled as to what they could mean.

Tommy studied the numbers. "They must be important," he thought, "preserved on this fine material." Then it occurred to him. He looked over at the safe and smiled. The safe was about six feet tall and three feet wide. The door had a large dial on the front, next to a steel handle. The dial had a series of lines and numbers from 0 to 35. Tommy began to spin the dial.

"Right, eleven," he turned the dial clockwise, stopping on eleven. "Left, thirty-one," he turned the dial counter-clockwise, stopping on thirty-one. "Right, twenty-five," he stopped the dial on twenty-five.

Click.

Tommy pushed down on the handle and it released. He pulled the heavy door open very slowly.

There before him was the largest treasure he had ever seen. Stacks of gold bars, coins, bills, envelopes of documents, leather bound books, all neatly placed inside the safe.

He turned and looked over his shoulder at the dead crewman wrapped in the blanket. He looked beyond the stacks of crates in the storeroom and listened instinctively for any movement.

He quickly turned back to the safe and began stuffing the pockets of the coat with one ounce gold bars. There were so many, he guessed to be around ten pounds of gold. Behind the stacks gold bars was a box. It was a fine cedar box with a gold latch. He released the latch and opened the lid. Inside the box were gemstones, the likes of Tommy had never seen. Diamonds, rubies, garnets, emeralds, some loose, others attached to beautiful works of gold. He filled what little room he had left in the jacket with the jewelry.

He stopped after taking enough gold and jewelry to last him a lifetime, as far as he was concerned. He left the papers and bills and smaller denominations of coins. In the back corner of the safe was a musket. The craftsmanship was remarkable. Tommy reached in and took it out. It was the finest gun he had ever seen. He placed the musket on the back wall of the storeroom. He took the pistol from the top of the safe and placed it next to the musket. Tommy walked over to the dead man and grabbed him by the feet. He dragged the body over to the front of the safe. It took some effort, but he was able to stuff the dead crewman inside the safe. Tommy took out the silk handkerchief on which the combination was written and tossed it inside. He closed the door and locked the safe back up.

Tommy started thinking about how he was going to escape the steamboat without being seen. Dawn was approaching and he wanted to leave before the sun came up. He prepared the pistol and musket by loading them with powder and lead he retrieved from a crate he had found earlier.

He began to hear rustling and footsteps coming from the deck above him. "Am I too late?" he thought, "the crew roused this early? Should I hide or make a swim for it?" He looked himself over and debated whether the jacket was too heavy and if he could swim with it on.

Suddenly, there was shouting from up above him, the words were indistinguishable. There seemed to be unexpected chaos and panic on the deck above. Then he heard a man shout, "Crenshaw!", the voice was coming from the stairwell that leads down to the slave's quarters. "Crenshaw!" again only louder.

Tommy aimed the long musket at the door that separated the back of the slave's quarters from the storeroom. He stood at the end of the aisle with his back against the wall that divided the storeroom from the boiler and engine room. He could hear the steamer accelerate along with the panic on the deck above.

"Crenshaw! To arms!" the voice demanded as the door burst open. "Bushwhackers!" the man yelled as he came through the door.

The man peered down the aisle at Tommy.

"Crenshaw?"

Tommy pulled the trigger and the gun fired. The lead ball lodged in the man's temple. The man reached up in disbelief as he felt the wound.

"It's me, Crenshaw, just me," the man whimpered as he collapsed on the floor.

Before Tommy could move, gunfire broke out from the upper decks. Tommy dropped the spent musket onto the floor. A thunderous boom echoed throughout the hull of the steamer. Tommy impulsively dropped to his knees. The ship shook hard.

"Cannons!" Tommy thought to himself.

Boom! Again went the sound. He could hear the projectile rip through the timber on the deck above him. Then an enormous explosion followed another *BOOM!* The cannon ball had punctured the boiler. Under intense pressure the boiler exploded, sending shards of metal and thousands of gallons of steaming water in every direction. The wall directly behind Tommy splintered into pieces and the storeroom filled with scalding water.

Like a rat that had fallen into a kettle of boiling soup, Tommy was being stewed alive.

RAWHEAD

The bubbling hot water engulfed him. It instantly soaked through his clothes and melted his skin. The pain was inconceivable. His entire body felt like it was on fire. His face and hands blistered, he struggled blindly to escape the cauldron of hell that was consuming him. He finally succumbed to the torture, sinking down into the darkness.

8 IMMORTAL CURSE

Darkness.

Silence.

Tommy felt nothing. He could not tell if his eyes were open or closed. "Breathing? Am I breathing?" he thought. He focused his mind and listened for his own heartbeat. He felt nothing. He heard nothing. He remembered nothing. His thoughts were empty. Darkness. Silence.

He was aware of his existence. His mind was cloudy. Clouds.
The darkness was changing. The clouds were slowly moving in his mind's eye. At first they were dark and menacing, fading in and out of the blackness, battling to break through. Like smoke swirling in the night, the grey began to change to white.
Light.

Tommy perceived a vision in his mind. He was standing in the middle of a room. Sitting across from him was a man. The man had a painted face. His face was white from his hairline to his lips. He was blood red from his lips down to his neck. His eyes were distant as if he was in the deepest of thought. He wore a headdress made of seven eagle feathers. His long black hair was intertwined with snakes of grey. Raven feathers also adorned his shoulders and the sleeves of his tunic.

"Who...are you?" Tommy asked.

"I am called Death Talker."

The shaman's hollow eyes looked past Tommy.

"Where am I?" asked Tommy.

"You are crossing over. Your body is dying. Your spirit has found me. I have been chosen to console with you. First, you must reveal yourself to me."

The shaman stood up slowly. He raised his arms out, spreading his raven wings. His yellow eyes focused on Tommy for the first time. The shaman became troubled. He fanned his wings and stomped on the floor.

"The Great Spirit has abandoned you to darkness! Evil and murder has consumed you! You are no longer human! Demon! I see you now!"

The shaman glared at Tommy and hissed.

"I have the power to guide your condemned soul back to your undead body, where you will crawl the earth in pain and hunger, a servant of evil forever, never living, never dying!"

The shaman stomped his feet and fanned his wings again. Then he abruptly stopped and closed his eyes. After pausing a moment, Death Talker calmly spoke.

"Your spirit is crossing over. You may let it continue the journey and learn of what awaits you on the other side...of that I do not see. I have spoken. What is your decision?"

"Return me to my body," Tommy whispered.

Death Talker closed his wings and concealed his face. The room became increasingly brighter. The shaman slowly disappeared, along with the furniture and the walls of the room until pure whiteness was all Tommy could see. The whiteness surrounded him. His senses gradually returned and he began to hear voices.

"We've done all we could do, he is just not responding, I am afraid he is dying."

"I understand that, Doctor Cooley, but it is very important we keep him alive."

"Colonel, with all due respect, I am spread out too thin here. I have several other patients that have a much better chance of survival than he does. This man has suffered severe scalding over his entire body. It is a miracle he is still alive and managed to survive this long."

"This man is the most valuable person in this building, doctor, we have gone through great lengths to bring him here to you. It is in your best interest to keep him alive and get him talking!"

"I cannot guarantee he will ever speak, let alone live through the night. But, I do have one final option..."

"Good, I hate running out of options. You had better get to it, and if it doesn't work, come up with other options!"

"Ok, bring him in!" the doctor yelled.

Tommy could hear scuffling and footsteps as the two men stopped the conversation. He could sense a third person had entered the room.

"He is known as Death Talker. We were told he can communicate with the dead," said the doctor.

"Can he speak English?" the colonel asked sarcastically.

"A little," answered the doctor, "although, he doesn't speak to the dead by means of *talking*."

The colonel chuckled despite the seriousness of the matter.

"You brought me a native that speaks to the dead! Tell him to ask if he remembers the combination!"

The room was quiet for a moment.

"I have already spoken with him," Death Talker commented in a solemn tone.

"What are you saying?" asked Dr. Cooley.

"He is crossing over. His spirit found me while I was waiting in the adjoining room. He wants to return to his body."

Tommy could hear the colonel moaning incredulously.

"The Great Spirit has rejected him," the shaman continued, "he is no longer man, but a demon in human form. It brings me much sorrow. The spirits elected me to guide him back. Here, you must give him this."

"What is it?" asked the doctor.

"Venom of the serpent..." the shaman replied.

"It better not kill him!" warned the colonel.

Death Talker answered, "No, it will not kill *him*, however, *death*, death will still come, come to you all."

Tommy could feel the venom flowing through his veins, igniting all his senses. The sting awakened his body. He felt his arms and legs fill up with poison. He felt the venom flow through the tips of his fingers and toes, although he could not move. The venom filled his eyes and they burned. His vision returned. He was lying on a bed. His entire body was wrapped in bandages. The poison surged through his brain causing him to shriek. The scream came from deep inside his body and worked its way up his throat and out of his parched mouth. It was as if the howl was not his but originated from something else.

As the scream passed out of Tommy's mouth, it forced his jaw open and split the stiff flesh of his cheeks. Blood filled the bandages circling his head. The doctor leaned over Tommy and unraveled the bandages.

"Incredible! He's alive!" remarked the colonel. The colonel could not believe what he just witnessed. He stood at the end of the bed studying Tommy. His face was hideous. The scalding aged him. His body was gaunt to the point of emaciation, his shriveled skin pulled tautly over his bones. With his bones pushing out against his skin, his complexion the ash grey of death, and his eyes pushed back deep into their sockets, Tommy looked like a corpse recently disinterred from the grave. His lips were tattered and bloody. Unclean and suffering from suppurations of the flesh, Tommy gave off a strange and eerie odor of decay and decomposition, of death and corruption.

His melted skin was pale with a transparency that revealed his flesh underneath. His eyes were sunken and deep red. He had no eyelids. Dr. Cooley had previously cut the lids away because they had fused together. Colonel Mulligan turned his head. He could no longer stand to look at the monster.

"Thank you," the colonel said to the shaman.

Death Talker hissed.

"Do not thank me! You know not what you have done! This is not the man you think he is. Darkness and death will be released upon this earth. A great battle will be waged on this cursed ground. This demon will feed on the blood that will be spilled here. The spirits are troubled!"

Death Talker paused and let out a long sigh.

"My work is done. I must leave."

The shaman closed his winged arms in front of his face and walked out of the room.

"Mr. Crenshaw," the doctor touched Tommy's arm trying to get his attention. "Mr. Crenshaw, I am Dr. Cooley. You have been in my care for several months now. You have suffered severe injuries, over ninety percent of your body has been burned or rather scalded. You were involved in an accident aboard a steamboat. Do you remember?" Dr. Cooley leaned in closer and examined Tommy's eyes for light reaction.

"Can you hear me, Mr. Crenshaw?"

"Ask him about the safe!" interrupted the colonel.

"Patience!" Dr. Cooley glared back at the colonel.

"If and when he can speak, I will come for you. At this time I would like you to leave the room."

"Very well, but I won't be far," the colonel turned to exit, "there are a lot of questions that need to be answered," he said as an after thought.

The doctor focused on his patient.

"Mr. Crenshaw, if you can hear me, please open your mouth."

Tommy strained to move his jaw.

"Very good. Again, I am Dr. Cooley. You have been in my care since June. You are in good hands. We have established a hospital here in the Anderson house. You are in the custody of the federal army. We are in

Lexington, Missouri. Do you understand what I am saying."

Tommy opened his mouth a bit and tried to speak but nothing came out.

"You are very lucky to be alive. I had to surgically remove your eyelids because they had fused together. You have lost a considerable amount of weight and I am afraid your muscles have atrophy. It will be some time before you will be able to move. The nerve endings in your skin have been damaged and I believe you will not be able to feel anything. You must be careful not to sustain any injuries, for you may not even be aware of them."

The doctor leaned in and dropped saline into Tommy's eyes.

"Can you move your eyes?"

Tommy looked left then right.

"Excellent. I would like to ask you a few questions. Please respond *yes* by looking right and *no* by looking left. Do you understand?"

Tommy looked right.

"Very good. Do you know what year it is?"

Tommy looked left.

"It's September, 1861. Do you know who you are?"

Tommy stared forward a moment and thought to himself. He then looked left.

"Your name is Mr. Crenshaw, Carl Crenshaw. Captain J.C. Mason employed you aboard the steamboat *Sultana*. Do you remember?"

Tommy looked left.

"Do you remember anything at all?"

Tommy looked left. The doctor sighed.

"I have been feeding you intravenously. Do you think you can swallow some water?"

Tommy looked right. The doctor stood up and poured a glass of water from a jug that was sitting on a small table. "I will try and sit you up," Dr. Cooley said as he propped a pillow behind Tommy.

"Ok, try and drink this," Dr. Cooley brought the glass of water over to Tommy. He gently poured the water into Tommy's mouth. Tommy could feel the cool clean water rinse over his desiccated tongue. He could feel it cleanse his throat and wash down to his stomach. Without thinking, Tommy whispered, "more...".

The doctor stood up and walked over to the small table and poured another glass of water.

"Mr. Crenshaw, you are doing remarkably well. Hopefully, you will get your voice back."

Dr. Cooley smiled at Tommy.

There was a quiet knock on the door.

"Dr. Cooley, it's Father Butler," a voice said through the door, "I am afraid you are needed. There are two more wounded soldiers arriving any moment."

Dr. Cooley placed the water glass back down on the table and walked over to the door. He slowly opened it and invited the priest in.

"Father Butler, if you don't mind, would you please help Mr. Crenshaw drink some more water?" Dr. Cooley pointed to the glass on the table, "I will be back as soon as I can."

The doctor gathered a few things and left the room. Father Butler picked up the glass and turned to face Tommy. The sight of Tommy filled the priest with trepidation. The water glass slipped out of his hand and shattered on the floor.

Dr. Cooley was waiting in the foyer of the Anderson house. The house was a three-story, Greek-revival style house constructed by Oliver Anderson, a prominent Lexington manufacturer. Sometime around July, 1861, the Anderson family was evicted from their home, which lay adjacent to Colonel Mulligan's fortifications, and the Union garrison established a hospital there.

Each floor had four large rooms, two on either side of a main hall that divided the house in the middle. The grand staircase was on one end of the main hall and went up to the second floor. The rooms were full of injured soldiers. The main hall was the only space left to allow for additional wounded. Dr. Cooley had separated Tommy from the others and kept him alone and secret in an additional servant's room that joined the house on the south side behind the main rooms and above the winter kitchen.

Four soldiers entered the front door carrying with them two men on stretchers. Dr. Cooley began examining the wounded and directed the soldiers to place them on the floor of the main hall. Colonel Mulligan entered the house from the front door as well. Two other soldiers who were talking rapidly followed him.

"Price's men are advancing. We believe they intend to take the hospital." A soldier said to Colonel Mulligan.

"Attacking a hospital is in violation of the Laws of War!" the colonel exclaimed.

"Regardless, sir, we feel that is their intent. We must prepare to defend our ground," the other soldier added, "we expect them to be upon us by early evening tomorrow."

"We are well prepared. Our garrison has over two thousand men," the colonel reassured them, "you must find Commander Sturgis and tell him all you know."

The colonel directed the soldiers away and turned his attention toward Dr. Cooley.

"How is Mr. Crenshaw?" he asked the doctor.

Dr. Cooley looked up at the colonel. "He is recovering, amazingly well, he just may be able to speak. Just before I left the room, we had made significant progress. Allow me to attend to these men and then we will see to Mr. Crenshaw."

When Colonel Mulligan and Dr. Cooley re-entered Tommy's room they were shocked to see what was happening. Father Butler was hunched over Tommy and was attempting to smother him with a pillow. The priest was hysterical and was speaking in a tongue that no one could comprehend.

"Father Butler!" yelled Dr. Cooley.

Colonel Mulligan ran over to the priest and pulled him away. The priest fell to his hands and knees, cutting himself on the broken water glass. He crossed himself and looked up at Dr. Cooley and Colonel Mulligan.

"I have been a servant of the Lord my entire life. I never expected to meet the devil face to face. Evil dwells within this abomination, IT must be DESTROYED!" The priest leapt up and made one last attempt to strangle Tommy.

"Father, you are out of line!" Colonel Mulligan yelled as he wrestled the priest away and forced him out the door. "See to him," the colonel directed the doctor toward the priest, "I need to have a word with Mr. Crenshaw!"

Dr. Cooley escorted the priest away and Colonel Mulligan closed the door behind them. The colonel sat down in the chair next to Tommy. Tommy lay still as his eyes examined the officer.

Colonel Mulligan was over six feet in height and as straight as a lance. He had a strong, wiry, muscular frame, an open, frank Irish face, and dark hazel eyes as lustrous as that of an eagle. His hair was long, glossy and plentifully mixed with threads of gray. A heavy dark moustache and a nervous, energetic look, indicative of the dash, the abandon, that characterized the anxious, confident temperament, and completed the personality of James A. Mulligan.

"Mr. Crenshaw, I am Colonel Mulligan. Dr. Cooley mentioned you may be able to talk now, is that true?"

Tommy indicated "no" by slowly shaking his head.

"Mr. Crenshaw, do not be frightened. Your appearance is rather shocking and has offended Father Butler, but we mean you no harm. In fact, you are a hero..."

The colonel smiled at Tommy hoping to reassure him and calm his fears.

"Mr. Crenshaw, we have taken great care nursing you back from devastating injuries. We are proud of you. It is very important that you remember what happened the morning *Sultana* was attacked. Can you recall anything?"

Tommy struggled in his mind. He could not remember.

"Perhaps, if I tell you what I know," continued the colonel, "it will help you to recall the events of that day and most importantly, the combination to the safe. Do you remember the combination? Please, Mr. Crenshaw, it is very important to us. The combination...any numbers coming to you at all?"

The colonel shifted his weight in the chair, he was becoming slightly anxious.

"Mr. Crenshaw, you were hired by Captain J.C. Mason, aboard the steamboat, *Sultana*, as the ship's security officer. You were in charge of guarding the storeroom and the ship's safe. On the morning of July 17th the steamer was attacked by a small band of bushwhackers. They had a couple six pounders and crippled the vessel by targeting the boilers. I am afraid you are a victim of that explosion. Fortunately, we were able to salvage the *Sultana* and most of her contents. The remaining crew was able to defend her remains until our reinforcements could arrive. Our men were expecting the delivery at St. Louis and rode out ahead to stem any type of piracy. They arrived in time to fight off the renegades. You understand, the vessel was carrying supplies and information to a rendezvous point in St. Louis. Where we had a boat waiting to bring the shipment to me here in Lexington.

I was very happy to learn you had the initiative to collect all the gold and jewels during the attack. For that you are a hero, Mr. Crenshaw. We recovered the gold and jewels from your jacket and in return have saved your life. We are very grateful."

After the colonel stopped speaking, it all started to creep back into Tommy's mind. He could vaguely remember the events of that day. The horrors of the previous weeks were a faded nightmare.

Colonel Mulligan stood up and retrieved a second water glass from a shelf and set it on the table next to the pitcher.

"We are running extremely low on fresh water here, Mr. Crenshaw, every drop is precious."

The colonel carefully poured the water into the glass. He turned and held the glass up high.

"A toast! To Mr. Crenshaw!" Colonel Mulligan took a drink. He walked over and sat back down on the chair and slowly poured a small amount of water into Tommy's mouth.

"There's some for now, and if you feel like talking, you are more than welcome to have all you want."

The colonel sat the glass down on the floor next to his side.

"Now, Mr. Crenshaw, I do have a few questions. First, I must tell you, we were able to recover the safe. It wasn't easy and it took some time. Unfortunately, we have not been able to open it, or even penetrate it, yet. It is a *safe* after all! Mr. Linus Yale, *Junior*, especially designed it for the Federal Army...Impenetrable! "

Tommy felt paralyzed. The wrappings and bandages were binding his entire body. He had no external feeling. A burning sensation was pulsing inside his body. His awareness was growing and he was uncertain of the colonel's intentions.

"Unfortunately, the captain did not survive the raid. Beside you, Mr. Crenshaw, Captain Mason was the only one who knew the combination to the ship's safe. We have sent word to Mr. Yale in an effort to acquire his assistance. The lock, being a new design of his, has made it difficult for even my best men to crack. Please, Mr. Crenshaw, can you recall the combination? It is very important. The documents inside the safe contain important research, classified information, needed by the Federal Government in this time of war."

The colonel leaned in closer to Tommy's face and looked him directly in the eye.

"Do you understand me, Mr. Crenshaw? Think hard, try to remember. Also, I would like a better understanding of how you managed to pocket all the gold and jewelry, retrieve the musket from the safe and lock the safe moments before the explosion. There is a bit of confusion here, plus, the slave boy, do you know what happened to him? I understand your captain, *against our policy*, owned him. You must realize your captain was playing both sides of the fence, am I right Mr. Crenshaw? I have to assume you took the time to free the slave from his chains before the attack. Can you explain? It's all a bit puzzling to me."

Colonel Mulligan leaned over and picked up the glass of water. There was little left. He poured it into Tommy's mouth.

"That's all we have. I will give you a little more time to think things over. I am needed elsewhere. Let me just say, we are running out of beds here and it is in your best interest to remember that combination before my patience runs out."

The colonel stood up and returned the empty glass to the table. He turned and stood at the end of the bed and faced Tommy.

"I am going to send someone else in to help you with your memory. I can no longer dedicate any more of my time to you. Unless, of course, you have some answers for me *now*."

Tommy stared blankly at the colonel.

"Very well, Mr. Crenshaw, you leave me with no other choice..."

9 ASSASSIN'S BLOOD

Tommy was left alone in the room. He could hear the cries of the wounded throughout the house. It was the sound of torture. Distant memories started swirling through his mind. Specters of the dead were screaming in his head. The burning venom pulsed through his blood vessels. He felt his strength returning.

He was not sure how much time had passed since the colonel left the room. Minutes could have been hours. He could hear the exchange of gunfire in the distance. The distant sounds of war surrounded him. The cries of the wounded, the echoes of cannons filled the air.

There was a quiet knock on the door. The door slowly opened. A gust of wind blew in. Following it was what appeared to be an angel. The woman seemed to float across the floor and turned to face Tommy as the door closed on its own. The woman was extremely pale skinned. Her dress was flowing and elegant. It covered her entire body wrapping the beauty underneath. The woman looked at Tommy and began to speak in the softest voice.

"You poor creature. You must be experiencing the most pain. Dr. Cooley and I have done all we can to keep you alive. I have been told you obtained consciousness and I wanted to see you."

She paused as the sound of distant fighting interrupted her speech.

"Mr. Crenshaw, there is not much time left. The enemy approaches and our men will defend the hospital as long as they can. I am uncertain as to who may be the victor. I am worried that the hospital will fall into the hands of the rebels. If that is the case, all of our patients here may be killed, along with you, Mr. Crenshaw. The doctor and I have worked hard to help you all. It would be a tragedy to see our work go in vain. Please, Mr. Crenshaw, tell me all you know."

Tommy looked deep into the woman's eyes. He felt confused. He did not know what to say. He tried to speak. Any reply at all seemed appropriate, but all he could do was murmur.

"Yes, do try, Mr. Crenshaw, it will be ok."

The woman picked up the pitcher and poured the final drops of water into the glass. She leaned over and poured the water into Tommy's mouth.

"This is all we have left for you, I am afraid. Can you say anything?"

Tommy appreciated the water and gave a final effort to speak.

"Leave...leave...this place, death...death is coming."

Tommy could see the tears pool up in the woman's eyes. She returned the empty glass to the table and quietly left the room. She offered no salvation.

Tommy listened to the sounds of battle; he could sense panic and chaos growing in the Anderson house.

The next morning a stranger entered his room. Unlike the angel who had visited him the night before, there was a darkness surrounding the unknown man. He was extremely large. He was clad in a heavy leather riding jacket. His face was rugged and worn, scarred with battle wounds from distant past. The hat he wore seemed to be part of him. It was black leather with a medium brim that sat low on his brow. He stood at the foot of the bed and looked Tommy up and down.

"Damn, looks like the damage has been done. Not much left of you, is there?"

The dark man moved closer to Tommy's side and loomed over him.

"Mr. Crenshaw, I am the last chance you have, so listen closely. I work for Colonel Mulligan. They call me *Mister Black*. I do the type of work that Colonel Mulligan does not like to do. Let's just say, he doesn't like to get his hands dirty. You following me, Mr. Crenshaw?"

Mr. Black smiled an evil grin. He pulled out a rusted set of scissors from his jacket and held them above Tommy.

"I always like to start with the fingers, it usually does the trick. Sometimes people get to talking long before I cut the first one off, other times, that's not the case. In this instance, I will give you one chance to stop the charade and tell me the combination or you will lose them all, one by one."

Mr. Black reached into the bed and gripped Tommy's wrist. He lifted his arm up, bending it at the elbow. Tommy could feel his skin tear underneath the bandages.

Mr. Black opened the scissors and slid Tommy's right thumb into the jaws.

"Don't worry, Mr. Crenshaw, I keep these sharp. They should cut right through these bandages fairly easily. Once they hit the bone, well, it's a bit more difficult, but they haven't failed me yet."

Mr. Black increased the pressure and the scissors sliced down, separating the wrappings. He stopped when they hit bone.

"Any numbers coming to mind, Mr. Crenshaw?"

Strangely, Tommy felt no pain.

"Yes..." Tommy uttered.

"What's that, Mr. Crenshaw?" Mr. Black leaned in a little closer.

"Numbers, yes," repeated Tommy. "Thirty..."

"Speak up!" Mr. Black insisted.

Tommy whispered, "Thirty-one..."

Mr. Black leaned further down so he could hear well.

"Did you say thirty-one?"

"Yes, thirty-one," Tommy spoke quietly, "twenty-fah..." Tommy trailed off as he muttered.

Mr. Black smiled. He slowly placed the scissors back in his jacket pocket. He leaned in, turning to face Tommy.

"One more number, Mr. Crenshaw, and you may not die today."

"Fah, fah..."

Tommy stuttered and glared at Mr. Black.

"What are you saying? Four, five? Forty-five? Come on, Mr. Crenshaw, try to remember," Mr. Black moved in closer to Tommy, "one more number, don't let me down, one more number and this will be all over."

What happened next took the assassin completely by surprise.

Tommy lunged forward, opened his jaws and sunk his jagged teeth into the assassin's neck. He bit down hard and crushed Mr. Black's trachea. The big man gasped and grabbed at Tommy's jaw, trying to loosen the monster's grip. Tommy did not let go. He could feel the man's warm blood flowing into his mouth. It soothed his parched tongue. He felt invigorated. With a twist of the neck, Tommy ripped the flesh out of the man's throat. The assassin choked and gagged as blood filled his lungs. He gripped his hemorrhaging neck and gaped at Tommy with a stunned look in his eyes. He hunched over and his total weight came down on Tommy. His hat fell off and dropped down to the floor beside the bed. Tommy watched as the assassin drowned in his own blood. The man coughed and gasped, fighting to breathe. A fine stream of blood was squirting intermittently out of a severed artery in Mr. Black's neck. The dying man lay across Tommy's legs. Tommy sat up and sucked the blood from the wound. The red liquid of life revitalized Tommy. It filled his body with an empowering sensation. The feeling of starvation subsided. The squirting pulse began to slow and finally stopped. Tommy watched as the final quivers of life abandoned the assassin's body.

10 THE DEADLY DRIFT OF LEAD

A lead ball shattered the glass window in the room, alerting Tommy that the siege of the Anderson house had begun. With a renewed strength and energy, Tommy shoved the dead man's body off of the bed. The deceased hit the floor with a loud thump. Tommy swung his legs over the side of the bed and stood up for the first time in months. His legs felt strong, his senses heightened, he had never felt this alive. He picked up the dead assassin with surprising ease and placed him on the bed. He removed Mr. Black's heavy leather coat and slipped it over his withered frame. He carried the body over to the shattered window and pushed it out. It fell to the ground below. Tommy noticed the assassin's hat on the floor by the bed. He bent down, picked it up and placed it on his head.

Gunfire peppered the exterior walls of the Anderson house. As Tommy peered out the broken window, he could see the advancing pro-confederate Missouri Guard. They came as one dark, moving mass, their polished guns gleaming in the sunlight, their banners waving and their drums beating. As far as he could see were men, men, men - approaching grandly. Union soldiers were firing back from their place on the adjoining balcony of the Anderson house and earthworks below.

Tommy exited the room in which he had been kept for so long. He entered an adjacent room that was much bigger. The floor was covered with wounded men who were either unconscious or calling out for help. The suffering in the hospital was horrible. The wounded and mangled men were dying of thirst, frenziedly wrestling for water in which the bleeding stumps of shredded limbs had been washed, and drinking it with a horrid avidity. Tommy quietly crossed the room and left through a side door that opened to the hall at the top of the stairs. As Tommy descended the grand staircase, he could see Dr. Cooley frantically attending the injured soldiers in the main hall.

Dr. Franklin Cooley took in all he could find room for and gave them his skill as a surgeon, while his good wife supplied them with the attendance and care that a woman alone knows how to provide. The action of Dr. Cooley and the noble woman who aided him was not only humane, but in view of the surroundings, was heroic, requiring a courage and self-sacrifice in no degree inferior to the men who defended the hospital.

Tommy continued across the main hall unnoticed, a specter floating by. He walked out the large front door and down the steps of the front porch. Pure chaos surrounded him. The grounds of the Anderson house were beleaguered by Confederates slowly making their advance.

The Union men held their positions, defending the hospital on all sides. They had dug a series of trench works in the hillside to help protect the hospital. Their earthworks covered an area of about eighteen acres, surrounded by a ditch, and protected in front by confusion pits and by mines, to hinder the enemy's approach. The constant booming of cannons rang through the morning air. The clever Southerners had created a long breastwork of hemp bales. The rebels were hiding behind the large bales of hemp and slowly rolling them up the hill as they made their advance. The Union defenders poured red-hot cannon shot into the advancing bales in hopes to ignite the hemp, but the enemy had soaked the bales in the Missouri River on the previous night, giving them the desired immunity to the Federal shells.

The deadly drift of lead swarmed around Tommy as he casually walked across the battlefield. Caught in the crossfire, he could see the projectiles as if everything was in slow motion. The shot was piercing holes in the long leather coat he wore, but the musket balls passed cleanly through his body with no effect.

The battle raged on. The advancing rebels made great use of their breastwork. Slowly but surely, the Confederates gained ground. The defending Union men were falling one by one as Tommy made his escape.

He continued down the hill toward the advancing rebels and their movable hemp bale shields. The bales were very large, at least four feet wide and two feet thick. The men were rolling them up the hill, alternating movement, while laying cover fire. Tommy could sense the rebel's astonishment as they shot at him to no avail. A brave young soldier leapt up from behind his hemp bale protection and lunged his bayonet toward Tommy. As the soldier rapidly approached, Tommy stopped and reached into the leather jacket. He pulled out the assassin's old rusted scissors. With quick reflexes, Tommy hurled the heavy scissors toward the advancing soldier. The scissors flipped end over end. The sharp tips plunged into the advancing rebel's chest with a force so great the soldier was knocked backwards. He lost grip of his musket as he tumbled back down the hill. Tommy ran toward the fallen soldier, swooped down and took hold of the musket. With astounding strength, Tommy leapt into the air, jumped over the fallen soldier and landed atop a large hemp bale. Two other guardsmen were slumped down behind it. They looked up at their aggressor. Tommy appeared to be ten feet tall. He was a living corpse wearing the coat and hat of a killer. The blood soaked bandages wrapped his mortified bones, analogous to a mummy.

Tommy forced the bayonet down and stabbed one of the rebels in the shoulder. The other rebel, out of sheer terror, made a run for it, abandoning his post, he screamed out, "the devil is upon us, he is indomitable! Run for your lives!" Shots rang out from all directions; the retreating soldier was hit in the back and dropped dead. At the bottom of the hill, Tommy could see the wide Missouri River. The safety of the water called out to him. He dropped the musket and marched toward the water, oblivious to the hell fire around him.

Tommy arrived at the river's edge. Looking back up the hill, he could see the smoke and hear the powder bursts as the siege continued. It wasn't long before the rolling hemp fortification had advanced close enough for the Southerners to take the Union works in a final rush. Colonel Mulligan requested surrender terms just after noon, and had his surviving men vacate their trenches and stack their arms.

11 LOST IN LITTLE DIXIE

The smell of gunpowder filled the air. The smoke was clearing and the sounds of war had stopped. The remains of the fallen were scattered across the battlefield. Tommy examined himself. The coat he wore was riddled with holes. The bandages that were so carefully wrapped around his scalded body were shredded and bloodstained. He removed the heavy coat and leather hat and placed them on the ground. He sat down and began unwrapping the bandages. He started at his feet. He was happy to see that his feet were in good condition, considering the rest of his body. He remembered the new leather boots he was wearing on the steamboat. He credited them for protecting his feet from the boiling water. As he peeled back the bandages further up his legs, the condition of his skin worsened. It was burned, blistered and melted. His arms had lacerations at the joints where his skin had split open. He could see his bleeding bones. He unraveled the wrappings further, revealing his torso. Through his semi-transparent skin he could see the muscles in his body expand and contract. He was alive. He could feel the venom constantly pulsing on the inside. He felt nothing on the outside. He was alive, but somehow did not feel human. He could not see his own face, nor did he desire to.

Tommy stood unclothed and walked toward the open battlefield and the remaining dead. He searched for a fallen soldier that was near his size. It wasn't long before he found one. He bent over and picked up the dead Missouri guard. Tommy tossed the body over his shoulder with ease. Somehow, during his transformation, he attained a strength he never had before. His senses were heightened. His vision was crisp and acute. He could smell distinctive scents from great distances. He could hear the softest of sounds.

Tommy carried the body back to a spot at the base of the big tree. He could hear the water slosh on the banks of the muddy Missouri. He removed the clothes and dressed himself as the Missouri State Guard. He wrapped the dead soldier in his old soiled bandages. He dressed the corpse in the assassin's leather jacket and hat and propped the body against the tree.

Tommy searched the battlefield once again. This time he was looking for a hat and a weapon. He had to be quick, for he knew they would be coming for the dead soon. The scent of fresh blood led him to a soldier who had fallen behind. Next to the dead man was a musket. Tommy picked it up and removed the soldier's hat and covered his scarred scalp.

It was the heat of the day. The sun beamed down on Tommy. The glare drove him back into the shade of the trees along the riverbank. He stared out at the wide

Missouri. He wondered where he was and what was happening with the war that surrounded him.

Tommy began to feel weary. The sun was draining him. The assassin's blood that fueled him had diminished. In the distance, he could hear voices descending down the hill. It was time for the opposing forces to gather their dead.

Tommy pulled the rebel hat down low on his head, held the musket in his hands and eased down the muddy riverbank. He slowly waded into the cool water of the Missouri. He submerged his entire body. The water relieved the heat and loosened his taut, scalded skin. He had no need for breath. His lungs filled with water and it cooled him on the inside. He swam further out to the main channel and the current swept him away.

It has been said, *the Missouri River is too thick to drink and too thin to plow*, and for this reason, Tommy had incredible buoyancy. He allowed the river to take him wherever it may go. He drifted for days, floating along, gazing up at the sky. There were moments when he felt he was the only being on earth.

The river was taking Tommy back east as it cut through Missouri on its way to join the mighty Mississippi.

An irrepressible hunger awoke Tommy from his daydreams. He no longer needed to eat. He could not starve to death. Nevertheless, he was cursed to suffer the pangs of starvation, the burning pulse of a lost soul.

The meandering Missouri River had delivered Tommy deep in the heart of Little Dixie, a region of Missouri that followed hundreds of miles along the Missouri River. It was settled primarily by migrants from the hemp and tobacco districts of Kentucky, Virginia, and Tennessee. When the Southerners resettled in Missouri, they brought their cultural, social, agricultural, political and architectural practices. They also brought enslaved Africans and their descendants, from whom they extracted forced labor and thus accumulated wealth.

On average, Missouri's slave population was only ten percent, but in Little Dixie, county and township slave populations ranged from twenty to fifty percent, corresponding to the concentration of large plantations along the river.

Having rounded an expanded bend of the river, Tommy heard the barking of dogs and the clatter of many voices. From his vantage point, he could see the prominent appearance of a long table covered with dinnerware arranged in the open air. Just below the table, a number of dogs were sniffing and whining. There was a bustle among several slaves toiling about a small fire along side a quaint log hut. Tommy could sense that something extraordinary was going on. Tommy's curiosity and insatiable hunger incited him to swim closer to the clearing at the river's edge. He crawled out of the water, dragging his water logged musket and edged closer for a better view. The aroma from the table was alluring. Tommy inhaled the delicious scent. As he watched, two of the dogs broke their attention on the table and turned toward him. They howled and ran directly at him. He stayed low hoping not be noticed. It was too late. The hounds were upon him bellowing in a strange manner. They had a paralyzing effect. He heard a servant yell.

"Massah King, I believes a man been washed up in

yonder clearing. He looks to be a guardsmen."

The landowner and his wife, along with several of their guests, stepped out of the cabin. The remaining dogs had joined the others and surrounded Tommy. They were howling, growling and jumping sporadically. The dogs fearfully snapped at Tommy, but none dared get close for they could sense the iniquity deep within his rotting soul.

The landowner and his wife along with two other gentlemen approached Tommy. The other guests stayed back and remained curious about the unexpected visitor. Tommy remained hunched over on the ground. He heard the men call off the dogs.

"This is a strange occurrence indeed," said the landowner, "this man is wearing the uniform of the Missouri State Guard."

As the man spoke, Tommy slowly stood up. The wife gasped as she looked upon Tommy's hideous face. She turned her gaze away.

"Son, are you alright?" asked the landowner, "my name is Mr. King. Are you lost? You're a long way from your post."

Tommy did not answer. He looked past the perplexed group at the table set for a feast.

"What happened to you? You look to have suffered greatly. Are you in need of medical attention?" Mr. King winced at Tommy's ghastly appearance.

"I think he is hungry," one of the other men finally spoke, "we should escort him to the cabin and get him out of those wet clothes."

The landowner and his wife had invited their friends together for a quilting frolic. The interior of the log hut presented a singular scene. A square table occupied a great part of the floor. It was surrounded by a compact body of females, whose fingers were busy on the quilt that lay stretched out before them. Though neither the smartest nor the costliest, it promised, judging from the quantity of cotton stuffed inside, and the close compartments into which the latter was confined by rapid and successful gobble stitching, to be of real utility and comfort during the coming winter.

Silence filled the room after Tommy walked in. The women looked up at the unexpected guest. They began uttering comments under their breath.

"Ladies, please," Mr. King interjected, "he is a soldier fighting for a great cause. His contribution to defeating the abolitionist cannot be without reward. Let us welcome him. We have a bountiful feast, which the Good Lord has blessed us with. It would be a sin not to break bread with this brave guardsman."

Mr. King led Tommy to a small washroom in the back of the cabin. Once there, he gestured to some clean clothes neatly stacked on a small bureau.

"We keep spare clothing in the cabin in case of an extemporized swim in the river. Please, help yourself. You may hang your uniform on the quilt rack to dry. Please remove your hat and boots. I will see to it they are thoroughly dried and your musket cleaned. You are welcome to sleep here in the cabin after we depart to the main house. I will contact General Shelby on the morrow and notify him of your condition. I will try to arrange transport to Boonville, where you will find the closest guard regiment."

Tommy stood silent, but nodded his head in acceptance. Mr. King departed the washroom allowing Tommy privacy.

The meal that followed was plentiful and satisfying. It was devoured first by the female and then by the male visitors, with a marvelous rapacity. Tommy sat apart, waiting for his turn. He was much amused with the bustle of the scene. He watched the plates run the gauntlet from the table to the washtub. Next to the tub sat young slaves of all shapes and sizes, who all strove to act as preliminary scourers, much to the disappointment of the dogs, who whined, whimpered, scratched, and pushed their hungry competitors, annoying the robust female servant who acted as cook, and who, with lustrous visage and wide eyes, flourished her dishcloth over the tub in a fume of impatience.

Tommy sat alone and finished the meal of pork, chicken, corn, greens and warm bread. A young servant collected the fine china plate with extreme politeness. The wealthy plantation owners kept to themselves, gossiping steadily, oblivious to Tommy. The women returned to the business at hand. They all entered the hut and continued their diligent work on the quilt.

The meal was great sustenance for Tommy. It filled the emptiness inside his body but failed to satisfy his unexplainable craving for blood. Tommy sized up the men who remained outside. He determined it would be a futile attempt to satisfy his bloodlust. He quietly excused himself and walked to a private spot underneath and old oak tree.

The early evening hours slowly gave way to dusk. The guests were departing as Tommy watched the final formalities. Once the guests were gone, Mr. King approached Tommy as he sat under the oak tree.

"We are leaving for the main house. Our servant, Cilia, will return later this eve with bedding. I have also instructed her to clean your musket and polish your boots. I will return in the morning to fetch you. I hope you have a good night's rest."

Mr. King walked away and left Tommy to tend to himself. After the hustle and bustle of the large feast, the fishing cabin seemed deserted. Tommy explored the grounds. He detected the smell of cold blood. On the backside of the cabin hung several funnels, they were placed above an angled trough of sheet metal that drained into an old bucket at the low end. The funnels were used for butchering chickens. The chicken was placed upside down in the funnel and decapitated. Its blood drained down into the trough that led to the bucket. An uncontrollable urge overcame Tommy. He knelt down beside the bucket. It was half full of poultry blood. A family of flies defended their claim on the bloody feast. Tommy swatted them away as he lifted the bucket to his mouth. He lapped up the old blood with fervor. Once again, he felt empowered. The blood gave him an energy that no other substance could. He drank nonstop until the last drops fell from the bucket to his mouth.

The servant, Cilia, had returned carrying the musket, bedding, polished boots and dry uniform. Her first glance at Tommy made her scream out. His chin was dripping with blood. It trailed down his neck and was soaked up in the clean cotton shirt he wore. The fat African woman dropped the belongings and was panic-stricken.

"Lord have mercy!" she cried out, "you are a mad man...cannibal...Li Grand Zombi!" She pulled a charm out, which she wore around her neck, and flashed it before Tommy. "Li Grand Zombi!" again she cried.

A temporary paralysis overcame Tommy. He stood motionless and watched the woman. A protective aura appeared around her.

"Li Grand Zombi...Snake Demon! I rebuke you! Retournez Ã votre endroit dans l'enfer! Go back to your place in hell!"

She exposed the charm she held in her hand. It was a gold snake wrapped around a staff. She shook the idol in front of Tommy, as she did so, it sent him into uncontrollable convulsions. He began spewing up the blood he had so desperately devoured.

The large woman turned and ran back toward the path that led to the main house. In doing so, she released the hold she had placed on Tommy. He pursued her with great speed. She fell to the ground as her dress was caught up in her frightened feet.

"Restez loin le diable!"

She held the snake charm in a firm grip and waved it before Tommy. An invisible force tossed him aside. He flew through the air and landed several yards away from the frightened woman. Cilia yelled as she struggled to rise to her feet.

"Master King! ...Save me!"

Cilia's defense had a strange effect on Tommy and he stopped the chase. Tommy spied his belongings on the grass and gathered them up. He hurried to the log hut and frantically donned the Missouri State Guard uniform. He picked up the musket and placed it on a small bench. Tommy pushed a button, found at the pommel of the bayonet, with his thumb. The button released the spring locks and allowed the bayonet to be removed.

Bayonet in hand, Tommy stepped out of the cabin into the coming night. Expecting the men to return shortly, assuming they would search the river for him, he made his way inland and crept silently into the shadows of a large hemp field.

The hemp crop towered over Tommy. The rows were narrow with a highly planted concentration. The dense foliage reached out to Tommy, resembling the arms of dying souls grasping for the last thread of life before slipping into darkness.

The howling of hounds grabbed Tommy's attention. In the distance, he could hear their baying and the sound of horses galloping. He knew the thick cannabis would hinder their advance. He continued deeper into the field of hemp, the limbs closing behind him. He could sense that the dogs had picked up his trail. He debated whether to wait and slaughter the pack or continue on to avoid a conflict with the landowner and his mysterious servant, Cilia.

Mr. Rutherford King was a wealthy Southerner who moved his plantation to Missouri after years of farming had depleted the soil in the southern Louisiana Territory. He owned over five hundred acres along the Missouri River Valley. Mr. King also owned the largest number of slaves in Boone County, the total sum of fifty-two. Mr. King was well prepared in the matter of hunting down runaway slaves. Slave hunting and capturing was big business. Individuals and gangs roamed Little Dixie preying upon both runaway slaves and legitimately free Africans. Trafficking in human misery, these unscrupulous bounty hunters sold their captives to the Deep South.

Tommy struggled further onward through the thick rows of hemp. He could not see the end of the row in the dark moonless night. His momentum was not one of panic but he could not stop himself from falling when the ground suddenly gave way beneath him. Ten feet he fell before hitting bottom. A large pit had swallowed him up. It had been covered with stalks of hemp to disguise the gaping trench.

Tommy landed hard. The pit was dark, deep and wide. Tommy lost equilibrium and took a moment to stabilize. He could hear the hounds approaching and knew they would soon be on him. The cut hemp stalks that were the ceiling of the pit now covered the bottom. The branches were thick with leaves and made it difficult to move around. Tommy could hear subtle breathing that was not his own. He explored around in the muddy pit. The darkness surrounded him. As he pushed away the hemp stalks, he felt what seemed to be a large iron ball. Its sheer weight made it practically immovable. Welded to the ball was a heavy linked chain. Tommy followed the chain and found it was secured to a cold steel flat spring of an extremely large foothold trap. The trap was over six feet in length and the jaws were three feet across. The breathing sound became more rapid. Tommy could sense the warmth of body heat very close by. He could smell salty sweat and human blood. He peered into the darkness. The pure blackness gave way to shadows. Tommy could see the body of a woman slouched against the opposing wall of the pit. Her right leg was trapped in the hungry jaws of the morbid invention. The mantrap's serrated teeth had sunk deep into her knee, crushing her bones. The woman's dark skin camouflaged her body against the mud wall. Her breathing was sporadic as she lay in a state of semi-consciousness.

Tommy leaned over the dying woman. He reached out and touched her forehead. Her eyes popped open. They were dark glassy orbs without focus. She was lost in a distant dream. Tommy observed a faint golden aura begin to glow around her. The pale light exposed the natural beauty of her face and body. Her exotic skin was covered with mud that hid the many scars beneath. It was her face that mesmerized Tommy. Her distant eyes were wet with constant tears. Her hair was long and billowy black. Her lips were soft and inviting. She was young, more a girl than a woman. Tommy admired her mouth as it slowly began to move. A soft angelic voice recited a song that came from a faint memory:

> "When the sun come back,
> When the firs' quail call,
> Then the time is come...
> Folla the drinkin' gourd.

> The riva's bank am a very good road,
> The dead trees show the way,
> Lef' foot, peg foot goin' on,
> Folla the drinkin' gourd.

> The riva ends a-tween two hills,
> Folla the drinkin' gourd;
> 'Nuther riva on the other side
> Folla the drinkin' gourd.

> When the little riva
> Meet the grea' big un,
> The ole man waits...
> Folla the drinkin' gourd.

> Folla the Risen Lord,
> Folla the Risen Lord;
> The bes' thing the Wise Man say,
> Folla the Risen Lord.

Thinks I heard the angels say,
Folla the drinkin' gourd.
Stars in the heaven gonna show you the way,
Folla the drinkin' gourd.
Step by step keep a'travelin' on
Sleep in the holler 'til the daylight is gone,
Folla the drinkin' gourd.
Keep on travelin' that muddy road to freedom,
Folla the drinkin' gourd."

Tommy looked up at the night sky. The stars revealed to him the hidden meaning in her song.

"There's a good day comin' and it won't be long,
Folla the drinkin' gourd.
All God's children gotta sing this song,
Folla the drinkin' gourd.
Folla that river 'til the clouds roll by,
Folla the drinkin' gourd.
Step by step keep a'travelin' on,
Folla the drinkin' gourd.

Folla the Risen Lord,
Folla the Risen Lord;
The bes' thing the Wise Man say,
Folla the Risen Lord."

The aura surrounding the girl became brighter as her song faded away. She managed to smile as her eyes closed.

Tommy watched as the swirling radiance of her spirit ascended into the heavens. Freedom had come to her at last.

The hounds had reached the pit. Their bawling instantly stopped at the first scent of Tommy. Their canine senses detected the wickedness trapped in the pit. The four dogs turned and fled. Tails between their legs, they whimpered and whined with fear as they ran off. Tommy heard a startled neighing from two horses approaching the pit. The horses reared back, throwing the riders off and galloped at full speed, back the way they had come. Tommy could hear unintelligible cursing. He looked up at the opening of the pit, there was a slight flicker of flame. He could make out the silhouettes of two bounty hunters peering over the edge of the pit. One was holding a burning torch to help light the dark entrenchment. Tommy rested his right hand on the bayonet he kept at his side.

A bounty hunter called out, "Didn't git too fer, did ye? Ig'nant slave's got no sense...fine by me...jes makes me richer."

The bounty hunter turned to his partner, "How's we gonna git 'er out? Scar'd damn horses run'd off wit da rope..."

The flickering torch was not bright enough to penetrate the depths of the dark pit. The bounty hunter held the torch further over the edge.

Tommy could see the two men standing side by side. Without warning, Tommy leapt up the ten feet of mud wall in one giant bound. He grabbed both men, each by one leg and pulled them down into the pit. One man landed hard on the iron trap, breaking his ribs. He struggled to catch his breath. The other flailed about trying to stand on a broken ankle. He was swinging the torch hysterically. The flames ignited the dry hemp stalks that were used to cover the hole. In a rush, the fire swept through the pit in a raging inferno. The screams from the strong bounty hunters were pitiful. The men did not anticipate being caught in their own trap, nor did they expect to meet the devil waiting inside. The flames singed Tommy's clothes and circled his head like a fiery halo. Tommy loomed over the fallen men. He could sense pure fear. Their screams intensified, yet, they lay powerless, gazing up at Tommy while their skin burned. Tommy's lidless eyes reflected the merciless flames. Tommy smiled and exposed his bloodstained teeth.

The body of the girl was lifeless as the dry foliage surrounding her burst into flames. The fire swirled around Tommy. It slowly lifted him up and he ascended out of the blazing pit.

Once above ground, he pitched additional dried hemp stalks into the hole, feeding the fire. The flames roared upward. Tommy shoved in more of the arid debris until the conflagration soared high into the night sky.

12 ULTIMATE AFFLICTION

Three months had passed since Tommy escaped from Rutherford King's plantation. Fall turned to winter and Tommy could sense the biting cold, but even the coldest or hottest days had no effect on him. He had returned to the safety of the river, hiding during the day and hunting and foraging at night, for he did not need to sleep.

He partially satisfied his craving for flesh by eating animals and fish provided by the river, although the deep craving for human flesh was insatiable. Compassion and emotion had given way to beastly instincts. Tommy was a revenant, more a beast than a man, a sentient corpse that terrorized the living. He had lost all memory of his former life. Instinct taught him how to replenish himself with venom of the serpent, by capturing vipers and sinking their fangs into his veins.

Tommy witnessed the most widespread, prolonged, and destructive guerrilla fighting in American history.

There was a horrific combination of robbery, arson, torture, murder, swift and bloody raids on farms and settlements, pursuit of outlaws, and the hunting down of Southern sympathizers by the Federal scouting parties. The conflict approached total war, engulfing the whole populace and challenging any notion of civility. Tommy could appease his constant desire for human flesh by devouring the bodies of the dead that were left to rot all along the Missouri River valley.

Like a vulture circling for its prey, Tommy was always there at the battlefields waiting the aftermath. He avoided the warfare that surrounded him. He stayed hidden in the shadows and watched the ferocious slaughter with exuberance.

The war along Little Dixie lasted four long grueling years. Tommy followed the fighting up and down the river valley from Boonville and back to Lexington. He made the Missouri River his home and over the course of time memorized every town, turn and tributary along the way. He always kept moving. He would appear out of nowhere, get what he came for and vanish without a trace. His reputation soon spread. He was known as the eater of the dead, a murderer of the innocent. People feared going near the river. The Federal forces battled the Secessionists for control of the river and rail that crossed the state of Missouri making the river and Little Dixie a dangerous place to be. Tommy had to be on close guard for soldiers, the constant patrolling of bounty hunters searching for runaway slaves, strangers of all types, for he knew he was being hunted as well.

The one threat he did not foresee was the native tribes, the forgotten people, the ones who knew the secrets of the land more than anyone else.

Tommy resurfaced at a fish camp along the big bend of the Missouri River. The alluring smell of fish cooking over an open fire drew him in. He watched as a young native woman tended to the fire. He could hear the laughter of youthful play hidden in the tall grasses nearby. It was early evening and the sun was slowly dipping below the horizon, casting long shadows of trees along the river's edge. Tommy kept his head slightly above the water. He listened and watched closely as the sound of the children became louder. The squaw attending to the fire was distracted, concentrating on the preparation of fish. Tommy waited silently as the insatiable hunger grew within him. It had been several days since his last taste of blood and the craving deep inside was maddening.

Out of the tall grass appeared two young native children. They were slightly out of breath from running in the field above the riverbank. Their mother called out to them but they didn't hear her. The two boys ran past her and jumped into the cool water. The squaw ran over to the bank and angrily called out again. Several moments passed before one boy resurfaced and was laughing hysterically. He swam over to his mother on the bank and continued to laugh. He pointed out to the water and waited as he and his mother looked into the river. He stopped laughing after realizing that his brother was not resurfacing. The young boy looked at his mother as she began to yell out once more. The squaw frantically ran into the water as she called out. She began searching, diving under multiple times to no avail. The boy was gone.

RAWHEAD

Tommy found a quiet spot along the river, hidden from view as he laid the young boy's drowned body down on the ground. He was excited to taste the fresh young flesh, used to eating the dead soldiers, a child was such a delicacy. Tommy slid the long bayonet blade out and cut the leather clothing away from the child. He examined the boy's body and admired the calves and thighs. He carved the meat right off the bone. He slowly bit down into the tender thigh, savored the flavor and absorbed the young blood into his ghastly tongue.

Relishing the moment of his latest kill, Tommy was caught unaware of his surroundings. As he sliced off another bit of the child's flesh he heard the screaming sounds of a war cry. Before he knew it was upon him, a band of braves were on the attack. A search party was sent out to hunt for the lost boy and startled Tommy as he devoured his rare meal. Out of the shadows came warriors with painted faces. They were advancing from every direction. Tommy was surrounded. The first arrow caught Tommy by surprise as it plunged into his side. It caused him to drop his bayonet and the meat of his prey. Tommy turned in the direction from where it came and another arrow pierced his chest. Before he could react they were upon him. Raging madness appeared in their eyes as four braves clubbed Tommy with their hatchets. Others appeared and had long spears with flint tips, which they thrust into his body. The savages had overwhelmed him and relentlessly pummeled him. Several men overpowered him and forced him to the ground. They held him down while others stripped him of his clothing and beat his bones with large rocks. Tommy looked up from his prone position on the ground and could see a large knife wielded before his eyes. The bearer of the blade let out a loud shriek and placed the edge on Tommy's forehead just before the hairline. With one quick slice the Indian removed the front half of Tommy's scalp. The scalper raised the trophy high above his head and screamed a cry of victory.

The savages continued to beat him and crush his bones. There were so many and the anger and rage they contained was merciless.

Then the dismemberment began...

They severed Tommy's hands and feet. They ripped his arms out of their sockets. They crushed his rib cage with large rocks found at the river's edge. They broke his legs into several parts. The raging savages pulled him apart like hungry wolves fighting over an animal's carcass.

Through it all, Tommy remained completely conscious. He watched helplessly as his body parts were tossed into the river.

He felt no pain, just a great anger.

Convinced they had slain the beast, with one final blow to the neck, they decapitated him. The severing of his head caused his detached torso to convulse. The Indians hurled Tommy's remains into the muddy river along with his retching head.

Several braves chanted and stomped their feet at the river's edge. Others attended to the remains of the child left from Tommy's meal.

A sudden gust of wind stirred the air and the chanting stopped. The braves all gathered together and watched as a figure appeared out of the darkness.

It was Death Talker.

"You are brave and mighty warriors," the shaman spoke to them in their native tongue. "You have avenged the death of this young boy. You are fortunate to have slain this demon here, at *Wakenda*, the land of the Great Spirit, otherwise, it would not have been as easy. You caught him at a weak moment."

The band of warriors silently stared at Death Talker.

"Young son of Red Hawk has crossed over. I have spoken with his spirit. He is not afraid and will join with the Great Spirit...give his body to Mother Earth."

Death Talker opened his arms wide and spread his raven feathers. His wings caught a slight breeze and he levitated over the riverbank. The warriors gasped.

Death Talker began to chant.

"Raw head and bloody bones, raw head and bloody bones, reveal yourself to me. I know you are watching us. Raw head and bloody bones! I feel your presence. I smell your stench. Show these brave warriors you have not been defeated so they will know who to fear!"

A gurgling laughter was heard as Tommy's skull bobbed at the surface of the river. It slowly rose up above the water and its eyes examined the mesmerized party on the shore. Under the water, the pieces of his body drifted toward the skull, wriggling and struggling to reassemble the living corpse of Tommy, known furthermore as *Rawhead Bloodybones*.

Death Talker flapped his wings hard. Rawhead rose higher. His body slowly lifted out of the water while it slithered into its proper form.

Death Talker suspended Rawhead above the river with an invisible grip.

"Rawhead Bloodybones! You are forbidden to enter this sacred ground! Your powers are useless here! Go back to the depths and disturb these people no more!"

Rawhead hovered above the river. His broken body appeared much larger than before. It vaguely resembled its former self. The anger and affliction he received at the hands of the savages only made him stronger. He looked down at Death Talker and began spewing blood and venom. The members of the scouting party dispersed rapidly, fleeing in every direction trying to avoid the poison that was raining down on them. The vomit burned into their skin. Death Talker closed his wings and shielded his body, releasing his hold on the demon.

Rawhead plunged down into the river and vanished.

14 ANATHEMA

"Rawhead Bloodybones is an anathema, an abomination, a being cursed by religious authority, rejected by God..."

Gramps looked up from the fire.

"He has been haunting this river and the town folk up and down Little Dixie for more than one hundred and fifty years. It's said, by the locals, what happened to the town of Wakenda, twice flooded in 1993 and 1995 and finally leveled by a tornado, was God cleansing the sacred area of the cursed Rawhead Bloodybones."

Gramps noticed the night had reached it darkest and coolest time. His story had gone on for a couple of hours.

Mack was constantly monitoring Will's breathing as he lay beside the two boys, listening to Gramps' every word.

Pops was the first to speak after Gramps had paused his long tale. "I heard tell of a creature down south, known as *Raguru*. In Louisiana, there is a story of a swamp creature, half man, half beast, like a zombie..."

"Zombies, swamp creatures, you guys are really having fun with this!" Mack interjected.

"My boy almost drowns and all you want to do is tell ghost stories! I am dead tired, but I think it's time we packed up this camp and hit the road!"

"Come on now," George spoke up, "if William was in bad shape we would have got him out of here. It just spooked you. Everything will be fine, Mack."

"It will be dawn soon, anyhow, and then we can leave," Gramps added, "I am too old to be tromping my way through the woods in pitch darkness, unless you intend on carrying me! Even so, I don't think we'd get very far!"

A small spattering of raindrops fell. Gramps tossed another bit of wood into the flames.

The young boys were comfortably sleeping close by and the men looked around uneasily.

"Another thunderhead approaches, should we carry them to the tent?" George asked.

"We could all turn in for a little bit," Pops wearily responded.

"No!" Gramps insisted, "we need to stay by the fire, it is much safer here. It will be daylight soon and then we can leave."

"Old man, you are starting to get on my nerves!" Mack barked. He stood up to stretch and at the same time a strong gust of wind blew across him, bringing with it large drops of rain.

A sudden lightening strike startled the group. The young boys were awakened by the loud crack and the following thunder.

"There is an old fire pit at the mouth of the cave," Pops directed their attention to the cliff behind them, "I suggest we grab the coals from the fire and what's left of the wood and move over there before it really dumps on us."

The men all agreed and started carrying the remaining logs and sticks they had gathered into the mouth of the cave.

"There are a few sticks in the fire we can keep, pick them up by the cool end and carry them over," Gramps instructed as he fumbled around for the small folding shovel he had brought.

"I can scoop up the coals with this shovel and lay them down as a base. Set the wood on top after I am done placing the coals."

Ben and Will sat up and watched as the men moved the fire.

"Can we just go home, now?" Will asked.

"Not much longer, we need to wait for daybreak. It is time you woke up and moved your butts over to the cave!" Gramps pointed through the darkness to the cave entrance at the base of the cliff.

They all had moved under the shelter of the cave just in time. The storm was unexpectedly violent and the rain was coming down in sheets.

"I hope it doesn't last very long," said Mack.

"Me, too," George responded, "plus, everything is soaked, so packing up wet tents will take a bit of time."

The men and boys stood around the newly relocated fire and stared out of the cave at the drenched camp.

"I'm hungry," Benny said, breaking the silence.

"How about some...*s'mores!*" George joked.

The boys excitedly looked at George and then frowned when they realized he was kidding.

"Not funny!"

George laughed.

"All of our food and supplies are in the coolers by the tents. We have one flashlight, a shovel and a fire. Who wants to go get the coolers, the other light and the ax?" Pops asked as he looked around at the younger men.

George and Mack looked back at him.

"We can't see two feet in front of us, let's wait till it lets up!" Mack responded.

"I wanted someone to get my chair!" Gramps griped as he squatted down on the dirt floor of the cave.

"I guess I will join you."

Pops sat down next to Gramps and the small fire.

George and Mack stood with their arms crossed and looked out at the rain.

"This is like watching paint dry."

George chuckled at his own joke and slapped Mack on the back.

They both stared out at the rain.

After an hour, Ben and Will were tired of watching the rain. They observed Gramps and Pops fight sleep as the old men twitched and blinked. Their eyes were heavy with age and barely open.

Their fathers were gazing blankly into the dark deluge as if to think that staring hard enough would make it stop.

"I'm bored. Let's do some exploring."

Will motioned to Ben to pick up the flashlight.

The boys slowly walked deeper into the cave and the walls gradually closed in on them.

"It's getting tighter down in here. I think we are getting closer to the end," Ben stated warily. He was a bit nervous about sneaking off.

"It opens back up. I am sure. I've heard this cave goes way back into the hill."

Will continued on. George passed him the flashlight and allowed him to lead the way.

The boys came to a narrow opening at the very back of the cave. Like a funnel, the walls of the cave closed down to a small point in the back. The gap was about two feet wide and four feet high and resembled a doorway. Will walked up closer and shined the light into the dark opening.

"Phew! It stinks in there!"

Will instinctively covered his nose with his shirt. Ben did the same.

"It smells like rotting meat...something dead," Ben concurred.

"It's probably a dead animal or something."

Will took another step closer and leaned into the hole to have a better look.

"Hey, it opens up again into a bigger area."

Will stepped through the gap and Benny cautiously followed.

The cave continued on. There was a small trickling stream seeping out from underneath the rock wall to the right of the boys. The water made a path across the floor and meandered into the dark shadows beyond the reach of their light. The air became thicker and the stench was even stronger.

The boys followed the stream. Will searched ahead with the flashlight. Ben was close behind with his hand on Will's shoulder.

"There! I see something!"

It was Ben who spotted it first.

"Bones!" exclaimed Will.

The boys turned and ran as hard as they could.

"Dad!" they both yelled.

Ben was first to make it through the gap, followed closely by Will.

"Dad!" yelled Ben.

"We found something dead! I saw its rib cage!"

Both George and Mack were standing in the same spot, their backs toward the boys.

Gramps and Pops were leaning on one another. Propping themselves up on each other's shoulders. Sleep had taken over.

The small firelight cast big shadows on the cave wall.

"Bones! We found bones!"

The boys were excited about the discovery and wanted help exploring it more, afraid to survey it alone.

George and Mack turned away from their hypnotic staring contest. Returning from a deep meditation, they had to focus their thoughts. By that time, the boys were upon them.

"Come, look what we found!"

Ben grabbed his dad by the hand.

"You boys didn't go too far did you?" Mack asked as he took a branch out of the fire to use as a torch.

"Let's see what you found. Bones, you say? What kind? Are they big, small...?"

"I think it's a deer," said Will, "maybe a wolf dragged it back in here."

Mack scanned the floor for any signs of tracks.

The boys ran ahead of the men and waited at the narrow entrance to the back cavern.

"I can smell something," George said as he walked up and took the flashlight out of Will's hand. He slowly stepped through the gap, followed by the other three.

"Over there! Follow the water," directed Will.

The men stepped forward. The cave was completely black. The flashlight's spot was barely cutting through the thick air, which reeked of death.

The light revealed an indistinct carcass at the edge of its reach. The ribs protruded up. The bones were picked clean. It was hard to tell from what animal they belonged.

George moved closer to allow the light to penetrate further into the blackness.

Will's torch was fighting to stay lit. The dense air finally smothered it.

George used the flashlight to peer past the carcass and followed the floor along the wall's edge.

He stopped.

"More bones..."

All four stared at the circle of light. It revealed a large pile of bones. There were bones of all types. There were several skulls from large catfish, antlers, hoofs, ribs, and spines. The pile was swarming with flies.

George moved the light up. As it traveled along, the stack of bones became larger. George stopped the light on what he feared the most, a small human skull, possibly a child's.

What first appeared to be a small pile was only the beginning of a massive collection of remains. The mound of the dead was higher than George's head, making it at least six feet high.

About half way up, protruding out of the eye socket of a second human skull was a long dark rod.

George reached up and pulled the object out of the heap of bones. It was cold steel. Similar to a sword, only shorter, it was triangular in shape from its center, tapering down to its rusted worn thin edges.

George turned and held it up in the light for all to see.

"It's a bayonet!"

Mack identified it immediately.

"We need to get out of here!"

George tossed the long blade down on the damp floor and it slid off into the darkness. He hastily led the others back out the narrow gap.

They ran along the dark walls, feeling their way as the cave opened back up.

As they advanced toward the fire, they noticed it was burning much brighter, the smoke was no longer leaving the cave as it had been before. The rainwater was rushing down above the cave entrance creating a wall of water. It was a surprisingly beautiful waterfall. The curtain of water was blocking the smoke from exiting. The smoke was slowly filling the cavern.

Gramps and Pops were standing up, frantically stoking the fire.

"You're going to smoke us out of here!" warned George.

"We need to leave anyway!" reminded Mack.

"Quiet!" demanded Pops, "he's just outside!"

Pops and Gramps both pointed outside the entrance to the cave.

Beyond the wall of water, through its transparency, they all could see a figure standing. Between the blurry cascade and just before the darkness, stood a looming disfigured skeleton form, watching and waiting.

"What are we going to do?" whispered Ben.

Before anyone could answer, the figure started to advance. Its arm was the first thing to pierce the sheet of water. Its left hand was twisted, the fingers a distorted mess. Gradually, the entire creature passed through the water, parting the translucent curtain. Surrounded by smoke and illuminated by the firelight, they could see the monster. It was a frightening, malformed creature with its rotten flesh barely clinging to its primordial bones. It had great height, even though it was hunched over. Its hair was long and wiry and grew out in different patches. It had a clear swath on top of its skull where no hair remained. It exposed a pulsing scalp with blood oozing from its pores.

Its eyes were permanently open, the large red orbs sunk deep in their sockets. The pupils were narrow slits. It scrutinized the men and boys with cautious curiosity.

"Rawhead," whispered Gramps.

"RUN!" exclaimed Mack as he scooped up the young boys under each arm. George was quick to follow. Mack charged passed the towering monster, carrying the boys through the sheet of rain. Rawhead twisted and lashed out. He let out a deafening roar followed by a spray of bloody venom.

Gramps and Pops took advantage of the creature's distraction and made a run for it. They hooked around Rawhead's backside and broke through the cascading water.

The darkness of night was giving way to the grey of dawn. The storm was still going strong. It was difficult to see the others. They were several yards ahead of the old men, breaking trail through the woods with great speed.

Gramps and Pops tried to keep up with the younger men, but their old legs couldn't move any longer. Gramps collapsed to the ground.

"Go on without me!" he gasped as he fell to his knees trying to catch his breath.

"George! Mack! Wait!" Pops yelled out to the boys.

Mack and George were still within shouting distance. Mack placed the young boys on their feet and directed George to take them to the truck.

"We don't know the way!" George exclaimed.

"Wait here!"

George directed Ben and Will to hide by the trunk of a large tree and then ran back with Mack to rescue Pops and Gramps.

The storm worsened. The rain persistently pounded the men. When they reached Gramps, they picked him up together, placed his arms over their shoulders and dragged him along. Pops glanced back toward the cave but could not see more than ten feet in the torrential rain.

"What about the camp, the tents...?" Pops asked.

"Forget about it and get moving!" George yelled.

Another roar from Rawhead reassured them that they were not out of harm's way. The creature was fast approaching, lurching after them, seething with anger.

"Hurry up!" yelled Will, "it's right behind you!" Will pointed passed the men as they approached him.

"Pops, you lead the way!" Mack insisted.

"We are losing Gramps!" George said as his grandfather passed out.

Gramps felt like he was running underwater. His mind was back at Omaha Beach. Everything sounded strange. His vision was blurred. The enemy was all around him. Lost in confusion, surrounded by fear, he could feel his arms over the shoulders of his comrades as they carried him to safety on the beach.

Gramps could hear the screams of the wounded and the cries of the fallen. The bullets whizzed by his head and the constant thunder of machine guns and mortars pounded unremittingly in his mind.

"We are going to get you out of here!"

He could hear the voices reassuring him.

"Not too much farther!"

"This will be over soon!"

"Hurry! Go faster!"

In his mind's eye, he could see his old Sergeant giving him a thumb's up, encouraging him to keep pushing on. He could hear his brave leader yelling over the din.

"We are going to kick their ass! Don't you worry! I've got your back! I am not leaving without you!"

The relentless chatter of gunfire drowned out the voice. Gramps felt his body being placed on the soft sand with his back leaning against a blockade. He rested and waited on the beach. He prayed for his boys to be victorious.

10 THE END

Gramps opened his eyes. He was lying on his back on a soft white surface. His son Francis, grandson George, great-grandson Benjamin, and their friend Mack with his son, William, were all watching over him.

"Is this my funeral?" Gramps coughed, "get me out of this coffin! I am still alive! You knuckleheads!"

"Relax, Gramps, we are at the hospital. You over did it a little at the fishing hole and we brought you here to get checked out," Pops leaned over his dad and touched his brow. "Are you feeling ok? Can you remember anything?"

Gramps tried to sit up. He wasn't strong enough to make it and collapsed back down onto the pillow.

"We won didn't we? The war...we won...I knew you boys would get it done. And you managed to bring me back with you, like you said you would."

Gramps looked around the room, "where's Sarge? I want to thank him myself," Gramps smiled at them, "yes, it's good to be back home," he closed his eyes and drifted back to sleep.

"We will monitor your grandfather for a few more hours," a nurse said as she entered the hospital room. "Everyone checked out fine. William is all clear. You boys must have had a rough night." The nurse looked them up and down. They were all soaked from head to toe, filthy dirty and smelled terrible. "Your grandfather should be fine, too. He is a little old for whatever *fishing activities* you all were doing, but having said that, he is in great shape for his age. He just needs some rest. I recommend you all do the same. Go home, get out of those wet clothes and get some sleep."

The storm raged nonstop for two full days. George and Mack waited until the flooding diminished before returning to the fishing spot. They brought with them an old school buddy who worked for the Missouri State Water Patrol and told him about the bones they had found in the cave. The officer brought his canine partner and was fully prepared to investigate the scene.

When they arrived at the hidden fishing spot, there was nothing to be found. The tents, hammocks, coolers, and things they left behind were gone.

"We had a fire right here!" George pointed to the ground where the fire was supposed to be, not even a trace of ash remained.

"We also had a fire over here in the mouth of the cave," Mack directed the trooper over to the spot. There was nothing, even the old fire pit was gone. The area where it should have been was flat and even and appeared to have been that way for years.

"Unless all the flooding mysteriously washed everything away, you boys are not in the same place," Officer Fredrickson commented.

"This is the spot!" George reassured him and shot Mack a puzzled look.

"I have been coming here for years! I know this is it! No mistake..."

Mack led the patrolman and his dog into the cave and directed them to the back cavern where they had found Rawhead's stash of bones. The trooper sent the dog in through the gap first and followed closely behind. George noticed right away that there was no smell coming from the cave. Everything was exactly the same except for all the things that were missing. The cave was completely empty; no bones, no huge pile of remains, not a trace of Rawhead or any evidence at all.

"There's nothing to report here, George," Officer Fredrickson looked up at his former classmates, "look, I have known your family for a long time and know you aren't the kind to be wasting my time with some sort of joke or something, so I will let this go unreported. You said it has been three days since you were here, correct?"

George nodded at the officer. He was completely perplexed. "Mack, you saw it too, maybe we should tell him..."

"Tell me what? Are you leaving something out?"

"No, it's just..."

Mack interrupted.

"No, it's just *not* what we *know* we saw the other day…if we think of something we will let you know."

Mack looked at George with wide eyes, fearing he may mention Rawhead and create an even more disturbing story that could not be explained. Mack directed the trooper back out the gap. Officer Fredrickson called to the dog and left through the narrow crevice. Mack turned around to look at George. George was searching intensely around the empty cave for one little shred of evidence to prove to *himself* it actually happened.

"I just don't get it…"

"Neither do I…come on, let's go home…"

George shook his head in dismay. He looked down at the floor of the cave where the small seep of water had carved a narrow path over countless years. His eyes followed the meandering fluid as it reflected the flashlight. The trickling stream was breaking up as it encountered an obstacle in its course. The water split as it followed the path of least resistance down either side of the object. George bent down and picked it up. It was rusted cold steel. He turned and held it up for Mack to see.

"The bayonet!"

AUTHOR'S NOTE

The story of "Rawhead Bloodybones" was told to me on the banks of Clear Fork creek in Knob Noster, Missouri, while I was being introduced to "noodling" by my neighbors, the Bentley family. I was around the age of thirteen at the time. Their two oldest boys, Rick and Doug were close to my age. Their youngest son, Travis, was just a baby at the time. Over the years, as he grew, we frightened him with stories of Rawhead coming to eat him. This book is dedicated to Travis for putting up with our torment.

Rawhead Bloodybones symbolizes death, whether a grim reaper in the water, or perhaps hiding in the closet. For that reason, this book is also dedicated to all the lost children that have fallen victim to evil or accidentally drowned. It is a cautionary tale, reminding all to enjoy life, separate myth from reality, stand firm in your beliefs, and take great care of each other.

The year of this story's first publication, 2011, being the sesquicentennial anniversary of the first battle of Lexington and the start of the American Civil War, I felt it was appropriate to include the actual accounts of the first battle of Lexington written by the commanding officers on the following pages.

Special thanks to T.R.

- *P.G. Swearngin*

THE FIRST BATTLE OF LEXINGTON

Fought in and around the City of Lexington, Missouri, on September 18th, 19th and 20th, 1861, by forces

UNDER COMMAND OF

COLONEL JAMES A. MULLIGAN, U. S. A.

-- AND --

GENERAL STERLING PRICE, M. S. G.

The official records of both parties to the conflict;

PRINTED FOR

THE LEXINGTON HISTORICAL SOCIETY

In the Month of May, Nineteen Hundred and Three

The Intelligencer Printing Company

The Lexington Historical Society was organized in September 1897, for the "collection and preservation of the original sources of the history of Lexington and vicinity," as the phrase runs in the charter of its incorporation.

COLONEL JAMES A. MULLIGAN, U. S. A.

COLONEL MULLIGAN'S STORY OF THE SIEGE

The following newspaper report (not stenographic) of a lecture by Col.
Mulligan was kindly furnished by Mrs. Marian Mulligan, who assures us that
the Colonel's official report never reached Washington.

- THE EDITORS -

INTELLINGENCER PRINTING COMPANY

On the 30th of August 1861, the Irish brigade of Chicago lay encamped just outside of Jefferson City. That night an order came from the General, at Jefferson City, for them to report at headquarters. Upon reaching headquarters the commanding officer said that the regiment of Col. Marshall, which had left for the southeast some days before, had reached Tipton, where they were hemmed in, and could neither advance or return, and that he wished me to go to Tipton, join Col. Marshall, take command of the combined forces, cut my way through the enemy, return to Lexington and hold it at all hazards. The next morning the Irish brigade started, with one six pounder, forty rounds of ammunition, and three days' rations for each man. Thus we marched on for nine days without meeting an enemy, foraging upon the country roundabout in the meantime for support.

We reached Tipton, but found neither Col. Marshall nor the enemy. The brigade passed on to a pleasant spot within two miles of Lexington, where we sat down, and made preparations to enter the town. We washed our faces, burnished up our arms, brushed the travel stain from our uniforms, and went gaily in with our little six pounder. Indeed, the trouble was not so much in getting into Lexington as in getting out. At Lexington we found Col. Marshall's cavalry regiment and about 350 men of a regiment of Home Guards. On the 10th we received a letter from Col. Peabody, of the Thirteenth Missouri regiment, saying that he was retreating from

Warrensburg, twenty-five miles distant, and that the rebel general, Price, was in full pursuit, with an army of ten thousand men.

A few hours later and Col. Peabody joined us. There were then at this point the Irish brigade, Col. Marshall's Illinois cavalry regiment, full, Col. Peabody's regiment, and a part of the Fourteenth Missouri--in all about 2,780 men, with one six pounder, forty rounds of ammunition, and but few rations. We then dispatched a courier to Jefferson City, informing the commanding officer at that post of our condition, and praying for re-enforcements or even rations, when we would hold out to the last.

At noon of the eleventh we commenced throwing up entrenchments. We had selected college hill, an eminence overlooking Lexington and the broad Missouri. All day long the men worked untiringly with the shovel. That evening, but six or eight hours after we had commenced throwing up earth-works, our pickets were driven in and intimation given that the enemy was upon us. Col. Peabody was ordered out to meet them, two six pounders were planted in a position to command a covered bridge by which the enemy were obliged to enter the town, and so we were prepared. That night the enemy, seeing our preparations, remained on the other side of the bridge, but it was a night of fearful anxiety. None knew at what moment the enemy would be upon our devoted little band, and the hours passed in silence and anxious waiting. Thus, we waited until morning vigilantly and without sleep, when someone rushed in saying, "Colonel, the enemy are pushing across the bridge in overwhelming force."

With a glass we could see them as they came. Gen. Price upon his horse, riding up and down through his lines, urging his men on. Two companies of the Missouri Thirteenth were ordered out, and with Company K of the Irish brigade, quickly checked the enemy, drove them back, burned the bridge, and gallantly ended their day's work before breakfast. The enemy made a detour, and approached the town once more by the Independence road. Six companies of the Missouri regiment were ordered out to meet them in the Lexington cemetery, just outside the town, and the fight raged furiously over the dead. We succeeded in keeping the enemy in check, and in the meantime the work with the shovel went bravely on, the diggers sometimes pausing in their work to cast anxious looks toward the graveyard where their comrades were engaged in the deadly strife, and yet the shovel was swiftly plied. This work was continued during the night, our outposts keeping the enemy in check, so that in the morning we had thrown up breast-works three or four feet in height. At 3:00 o'clock in the afternoon of the 12th the engagement opened with artillery. A volley of grape from the enemy was directed at a group of our officers who were outside the breast-works, which had an amusing effect. Every officer immediately sought the protection of the breast-works, and gained the inside of the lines of men. But this movement was attributed by them to the terror of their horses, not from any desire to contemplate the enemy from a less exposed position. Our men had returned the volley and a scene of the wildest confusion commenced. Each man evidently believed that he who made the most noise was doing the most shooting. Those who were not shooting at the moon were shooting above it, into the earth, or elsewhere at random, in the wildest, most reckless manner. This could not continue long with forty rounds of ammunition, and the men were ordered to cease firing, and were then arranged in ranks and instructed to fire with more precision, and carefully; and soon everything was in order and moved on as cleverly as a Yankee clock. This contest raged about an hour and a half, when we had the satisfaction, by a lucky shot, of knocking over the enemy's big gun, exploding a powder caisson, and otherwise creating a vast amount of damage, which was received with great shouts by our brave men. The fight was continued until dusk, and as the moon raised that great army of 10,000 men were in full and precipitate retreat, and Lexington was our own again. We resumed the shoveling and worked unceasingly through the night. Next morning Gen. Parsons, with 10,000 men at his back, sent in a flag of truce to a little garrison of 2,700, asking permission to enter the town to take care of his wounded and bury his dead, claiming that when the noblest soldier of them all, the lion-hearted Lyon, had fallen, he had granted every privilege to the Federal officers who had sought his corpse.

It was not necessary to quote any precedent to the Irish brigade for an act of humanity, and friend and foe met above the slain and together performed the last rites over the fallen.

On Friday, though a drenching rain set in, the work of throwing up the entrenchments went on, and the men stood almost knee deep in mud and water at their work. We had taken the basement of the Masonic college, an edifice from which the eminence took its name. A quantity of powder was obtained and the men commenced making cartridges. A foundry was fitted up, and 150 rounds of shot-grape and canister were cast for each of our six pounders. We had found no provisions at Lexington, and our 2,700 men were getting short of rations. Sunday had now arrived. Father Butler, our chaplain, celebrated mass upon the hillside, and all were considerably strengthened and encouraged by his words, and after services were over we went back to the works, actively casting shot and stealing provisions from the inhabitant's roundabout. Our pickets were all the time skirmishing with the enemy, and we were casting shot and making preparations for defense against the enemy's attack, which was expected on the morrow.

At 9:00 o'clock on the morning of the 18th the enemy was seen approaching. His force had been strengthened to 28,000 men, with thirteen pieces of cannon. They came as one dark, moving mass, their polished guns gleaming in the sunlight, their banners waving, and their drums beating--everywhere, as far as we could see were men, men, men--approaching grandly. Our earth-works covered an area of about eighteen acres, surrounded by a ditch, and protected in front by what were called "confusion pits," and by mines, to embarrass their approach. Our men stood firm behind the breast-works, none trembling or pale, and the whole place was solemn and silent. As Father Butler went around among them they asked his blessing and received it uncovered; then turned and sternly cocked their muskets. The enemy came, 28,000 men, upon my poor, devoted little band, and opened a terrible fire with thirteen pieces of cannon, on the right and on the left, and in the rear, which we answered with determination and spirit. Our spies had brought intelligence, and had all agreed that it was the intention of the enemy to make a grand rush, overwhelm us, and bury us in the trenches of Lexington. The fight commenced at 9:00 o'clock, and for three days they never ceased to pour upon us a deadly fire. At noon word was brought that the enemy had taken the hospital. We had not fortified that. It was situated outside the entrenchments, and I had supposed that the little white flag was a sufficient protection for the wounded and dying soldier who had finished his service and who was powerless for harm--our chaplain, our surgeon, and 150 wounded men. The enemy took it without opposition, filled it with their sharpshooters, and from every window, from the scuttles on the roof, poured right into our entrenchments a deadly drift of lead.

Several companies were ordered to re-take the hospital, but failed to do so. The Montgomery guard of the Irish brigade was ordered to a company, which we knew would go through. Their captain admonished them that they were called upon to go where the others dared not, and they were implored to uphold the gallant name, which they bore, and the word was given to "charge!" The distance across the plain from the hospital to the entrenchments was about 800 yards; they started at first quick, then double quick, then on a run, then faster-still the deadly drift of lead poured upon them, but on they went--a wild line of steel, and what is better than steel, irresistible human will. They marched up to the hospital, first opened the door without shot or shout-- until they encountered the enemy within, whom they hurled out and far down the hill beyond. The captain, twice wounded, came back with his brave band, through a path strewn with forty-five of the eighty lions who had gone out upon the field of death. We were now in the most terrible situation. The fire had hesitated for a little while, and the rebel commander had at once sent word to us that we must at once surrender, or they would hoist the black flag and show no quarter. Word was sent back that it would be time to settle that question when we asked for quarter, and then the terrible fire was resumed. Our surgeon was held by the enemy against all rules of war, and that, too, when we had released a surgeon of the enemy on his mere pledge that he was such. It was a terrible thing to see those brave fellows mangled and wounded, without skillful hands to bind their ghastly wounds. Capt. Moriarity, of the Irish brigade, who had been in civil life a physician, was ordered to lay aside his sword and go into the hospital. He went, and through the entire siege worked among the wounded with no other instrument than a razor. The suffering in the hospital was horrible. The wounded and mangled men dying for thirst, frenziedly wrestling for water in which the bleeding stumps of mangled limbs had been washed, and drinking it with a horrid avidity.

On the morning of the 19th the firing was resumed and continued all day. The officers had told our men that if we could hold out to the 19th we would be reinforced, and all through the day the men watched anxiously for the appearance of a friendly flag under which aid was to reach them, and listened eagerly for the sound of friendly cannon. But they looked and listened in vain, and all day long they fought without water, their parched lips cracking, their tongues swollen, and the blood running down their chins when they bit their cartridges, and the saltpeter entered their cracked and blistered lips, but not a word of murmuring. The morning of the 20th broke, but no re-enforcements had come; still the men fought on. The rebels appeared that day with an artifice that was destined to overreach us and secure to them the possession of our entrenchments. They had constructed a movable breastwork of hemp bales, rolling them before their lines up the hill, and advanced their artillery under this cover. All our efforts could not retard the advance of these bales. Round shot and bullets were poured against them but they would only rock a little, and then settle back. Heated shots were fired with the hope of setting them on fire, but the enemy had taken the precaution to soak the bales in the Missouri and they would not burn. Thus, for hours the fight continued, we striving to knock down or burn their hemp bales, and they striving to knock down our breast-works. Finally, the rush came. The enemy left the protection of their bales and with a wild yell swept over our earth-works and against our lines, and a deadly struggle commenced. Many heroic deeds were done in that encounter. Our men were encouraged by being told that if we succeeded in keeping them in check, this time we had them whipped; the lines stood firm. At this juncture we ordered up Capt. Fitzgerald, of the Irish brigade, with his company, to sustain the wavering line. Our cartridges were now nearly used up, many of our brave fellows had fallen, and it was evident that the fight must soon cease, when at 3:00 o'clock an orderly came, saying that the enemy had sent a flag of truce. With the flag came a note from Gen. Price asking why the firing had ceased. I returned it, with the reply written on the back, saying: "General, I hardly know, unless you have surrendered." He at once took pains to assure me that such was not the case. I afterwards discovered what the trouble was. A lily-livered man, a major by courtesy, ensconced under the earth-works, out of sight, had raised a white flag. Twice he had been threatened with death if he did not take that cursed thing down; but the third time his fears overcame his discretion and made for a moment a brave man of him, and he hoisted the flag over the breast-works on a ramrod. The ammunition was about gone, there was no water, we were out of rations, and many of the men felt like giving up the post, which it seemed impossible to hold any longer. They were ordered back to the earthworks and told to use up all their powder, and then defend themselves as best they could, but to hold their place. They obeyed, silently and grim. Without a murmur they went back and stood at their post, only praying that the enemy would approach so near that they might use the soldier's weapon, when his powder fails, the bayonet. Then a council of war was held in the college and the question of surrender put to the officers, and a ballot was taken. Only two of the six votes were cast in favor of fighting on, and the flag of truce was sent out. With our surrender, many of the brave fellows shed tears. And so the place was lost.

The enemy undertook to haul down our flag, and at first found the halyard cut; they climbed to the top and found it nailed. Their only resource was to cut down the pole, which was done while we turned our faces away. Gathering up the prisoners, the colonel in front, we were taken down to their camp and brought before a man in authority, who said we must promise not to "run away". We told him that we had not been in the habit of doing much of that business of late. Refusing to give our parole not to "aid or abet the United States", we were marched off prisoners, with General Price, and thus ended the siege of Lexington.

MAJOR GENERAL STERLING PRICE

OFFICIAL REPORT OF THE BATTLE

Report of Maj. Gen. Sterling Price, commanding
Missouri State Guard (Confederate), of operations,
September 10-20, 1861.

HEADQUARTERS MISSOURI STATE GUARD,
CAMP WALLACE, LEXINGTON, MO.,
SEPTEMBER 21, 1861.

I have the honor to submit to your Excellency, the following report of the action, which terminated on the 20th, instant with the surrender of the United States forces and property at this place to the army under my command:

After chastising the marauding armies of Lane and Montgomery and driving them out of the State, and after compelling them to abandon Fort Scott, as detailed in my last report, I continued my march towards this point with an army increasing hourly in numbers and enthusiasm.

On the 10th instant, just as we were about to encamp for the day a mile or two west of Rose Hill, I learned that a detachment of Federal troops and Home Guards were marching from Lexington to Warrensburg to rob the bank in that place and plunder and arrest the citizens of Johnson County, in accordance with General Fremont's proclamation and instructions. Although my men were greatly fatigued by several days' continuous and rapid marching, I determined to press forward so as to surprise the enemy, if possible, at Warrensburg. Therefore, after resting a few hours, we resumed the march at sunset, and marched without intermission until 2 o'clock in the morning, when it became evident that the infantry, very few of whom had eaten a mouthful in twenty-two hours, could march no farther. I then halted them, and went forward with the largest part of my mounted men until we came, about daybreak, within view of Warrensburg, where I ascertained that the enemy had hastily fled about midnight, burning the bridges behind them.

The rain began to fall about the same time. This circumstance, coupled with the fact that my men had been fasting for more than twenty-four hours, constrained me to abandon the idea of pursuing the enemy that day. My infantry and artillery having come up, we encamped at Warrensburg, whose citizens vied with each other in feeding my almost famished soldiers.

An unusually violent storm delayed our march the next morning (September 12) until about 10 o'clock. We then pushed forward rapidly, still hoping to overtake the enemy. Finding it impossible to do this with my infantry, I again ordered a detachment to move forward, and placing myself at their head, continued the pursuit to within two and a half miles of Lexington, when, having learned that the enemy were already within town, and it being late and my men fatigued by a forced march and utterly without provisions, I halted for the night.

About daybreak the next morning (September 13) a sharp skirmish took place between our pickets and the enemy's out-posts. This threatened to become general. Being unwilling, however, to risk a doubtful engagement, when a short delay would make success certain, I fell back two or three miles and awaited the arrival of my infantry and artillery. These having come up, we advanced upon the town, driving the enemy's pickets until we came within a short distance of the city itself. Here the enemy attempted to make a stand, but they were speedily driven from every position and forced to take shelter within their entrenchments. We then took position within easy range of the college, which building they had strongly fortified, and opened upon them a brisk fire from Bledsoe's battery, which, in the absence of Capt. Bledsoe, who had been wounded at Big Dry Wood, was gallantly commanded by Capt. Emmett MacDonald, and by Parsons' battery, under the skillful command of Capt. Guibor.

Finding, after sunset, that our ammunition, the most of which had been left behind on the march from Springfield, was nearly exhausted, and that my men, thousands of whom had not eaten a particle in thirty-six hours, required rest and food, I withdrew to the fair ground and encamped there. My ammunition wagons having been at last brought up, and large re-enforcements having been received, I again moved into town on Wednesday, the 18th instant, and began the final attack on the enemy's works.

Brigadier-General Rains' division occupied a strong position on the east and northeast of the fortifications, from which an effective cannonading was kept up on the enemy by Bledsoe's battery, under command, except on the last day, of Capt. Emmett MacDonald, and another battery, commanded by Capt. Churchill Clark, of Saint Louis. Both these gentlemen, and the men and officers under their command, are deservedly commended in accompanying report of Brigadier-General Rains. Gen. Parsons took a position southwest of the works, whence his battery, under command of Capt. Guibor, poured a steady fire into the enemy. Skirmishers and sharpshooters were also sent forward from both of these divisions to harass and fatigue the enemy, and to cut them off from the water on the north, east, and south of the college, and did inestimable service in the accomplishment of these purposes.

Col. Congreve Jackson's division and a part of Gen. Steele's were posted near Gens. Rains' and Parsons' as a reserve, but no occasion occurred to call them into action. They were, however, at all times vigilant and ready to rush upon the enemy.

Shortly after entering the city on the 18th, Col. Rives, who commanded the Fourth Division in the absence of Gen. Slack, led his regiment and Col. Hughes' along the river bank to a point immediately beneath and west of the fortifications, Gen. McBride's command and a portion of Col. (Gen.) Harris' having been ordered to re-enforce him. Col. Rives, in order to cut off the enemy's means of escape, proceeded down the bank of the river to capture a steamboat, which was lying just under their guns. Just at this moment a heavy fire was opened upon him from Col. Anderson's large dwelling house on the summit of the bluffs, which the enemy were occupying as a hospital, and upon which a white flag was flying.

Several companies of Gen. Harris' command and the gallant soldiers of the Fourth Division, who have won upon so many battlefields the proud distinction of always being among the bravest of the brave, immediately rushed upon and took the place. The important position thus secured was within 125 yards of the enemy's entrenchments. A company from Col. Hughes' regiment then took possession of the boats, one of which was richly freighted with valuable stores.

Gen. McBride's and Gen. Harris' divisions meanwhile gallantly stormed and occupied the bluffs immediately north of Anderson's house. The possession of these heights enabled our men to harass the enemy so greatly that, resolving to regain them, they made upon the house a successful assault, and one which would have been honorable to them had it not been accompanied by an act of savage barbarity - the cold-blooded and cowardly murder of three defenseless men, who had laid down their arms and surrendered themselves as prisoners.

The position thus retaken by the enemy was soon regained by the brave men who had been driven from it, and was thenceforward held by them to the very end of the contest. The heights to the left of Anderson's house, which had been taken, as before stated, by Gens. McBride and Harris and by part of Steele's command, under Col. Boyd and Maj. Winston, were rudely fortified by our soldiers, who threw up breast-works as well as they could with their slender means.

On the morning of the 20th, instant, I caused a number of hemp bales to be transported to the river heights, where moveable breastworks were speedily constructed out of them by Gens. Harris and McBride, Col. Rives, Maj. Winston, and their respective commands. Capt. Kelley's battery (attached to Gen. Steele's division) was ordered at the same time to the position occupied by Gen. Harris' force and quickly opened a very effective fire, under the direction of its gallant captain, upon the enemy. These demonstrations, and particularly the continued advance of the hempen breastworks, which were as efficient as the cotton bales at New Orleans, quickly attracted the attention and excited the alarm of the enemy, who made many daring attempts to drive us back. They were, however, repulsed in every instance by the unflinching courage and fixed determination of our men. In these desperate encounters the veterans of McBride's and Slack's divisions fully sustained their proud reputation, while Col. Martin Green and his command, and Col. Boyd and Maj. Winston and their commands, proved themselves worthy to fight by the side of the men who had by their courage and valor won imperishable honor in the bloody battle of Springfield.

After 2 o'clock in the afternoon of the 20th, and after fifty-two hours of continuous firing, a white flag was displayed by the enemy on that part of the works nearest to Col. Green's position, and shortly afterwards another was displayed opposite to Col. Rives'. I immediately ordered a cessation of all firing on our part, and sent forward one of my staff officers to ascertain the object of the flag and to open negotiations with the enemy if such should be their desire. It was finally, after some delay, agreed by Col. Marshall and the officers associated with him for that purpose by Col. Mulligan, that the United States forces should lay down their arms and surrender themselves as prisoners of war to this army. These terms having been made known were ratified by me and immediately carried into effect.

Our entire loss in this series of engagements amounts to 25 killed and 72 wounded. The enemy's loss was much greater.

The visible fruits of this almost bloodless victory are very great; about 3,500 prisoners, among whom are Cols. Mulligan, Marshall, Peabody, White and Grover, Maj. Van Horn, and 118 other commissioned officers, 5 pieces of artillery and two mortars, over 3,000 stands of infantry arms, a large number of sabers, about 750 horses, many sets of cavalry equipments, wagons, teams, and ammunition, more than $100,000 worth of commissary stores, and a large amount of other property. In addition to all this, I obtained the restoration of the great seal of the State and the public records, which had been stolen from their proper custodian, and about $900,000 in money, of which the bank at this place bad been robbed, and which I have caused to be returned to it.

This victory has demonstrated the fitness of our citizen soldiers for the tedious operations of a siege as well as for a dashing charge. They lay for fifty-two hours in the open air without tents or covering, regardless of the sun and rain and in the very presence of a watchful and desperate foe, manfully repelling every assault and patiently awaiting any orders to storm the fortifications. No general ever commanded a braver or a better army. It is composed of the best blood and the bravest men of Missouri.

Where nearly every one, officers and men, behaved so well, as is known to your Excellency, who was present with the army during the whole period embraced in this report, it is impossible to make special mention of individuals without seemingly making invidious distinctions; but I may be permitted to express my personal obligations to my volunteer aides, as well as my staff, for their efficient services and prompt attention to all my orders.

I have the honor to be, with the greatest respect, your Excellency's obedient servant,

STERLING PRICE, Major General, Commanding.

Hon. C. F. Jackson, Governor of the State of Missouri.

The Anderson House, Lexington, Missouri, was heavily damaged by cannon and musket balls during the first battle of Lexington. Many of the holes are still visible today. The house is a historical landmark maintained by the Missouri Department of Natural Resources.

ABOUT THE AUTHOR

Philip G. Swearngin holds a Bachelor of Science Degree in Broadcasting and Film from the University of Central Missouri. He has worked as a writer, producer, editor and director at radio and television stations in Missouri, Colorado, Alaska and California. He worked over twelve years with Fox Sports Television Networks in Los Angeles as a Producer, Editor and Director of national and international sports promotions and program content. He is the writer and producer of "The Carpetbagger Project – Secret Heroes", a World War II documentary on The Military Network. He lives in Missouri with his wife, Melissa and son Jackson, telling stories as an author and independent filmmaker.

CPSIA information can be obtained
at www.ICGtesting.com
Printed in the USA
BVOW10s0750020417
480078BV00016B/832/P

9 781463 762278